Getting to Third Date

How Not to Spend Your Senior Year
BY CAMERON DOKEY

Royally Jacked
BY NIKI BURNHAM

Ripped at the Seams
BY NANCY KRULIK

Spin Control
BY NIKI BURNHAM

Cupidity
BY CAROLINE GOODE

South Beach Sizzle
BY SUZANNE WEYN AND DIANA GONZALEZ

She's Got the Beat
BY NANCY KRULIK

30 Guys in 30 Days
BY MICOL OSTOW

Animal Attraction
BY JAMIE PONTI

A Novel Idea
BY AIMEE FRIEDMAN

Scary Beautiful
BY NIKI BURNHAM

Getting to Third Date

KELLY McCLYMER

Simon Pulse

New York London Toronto Sydney

This book is a work of fiction. Any references to historical events, real people, or real locales are used fictitiously. Other names, characters, places, and incidents are the product of the author's imagination, and any resemblance to actual events or locales or persons, living or dead, is entirely coincidental.

SIMON PULSE
An imprint of Simon & Schuster Children's Publishing Division
1230 Avenue of the Americas, New York, NY 10020

Copyright © 2006 by Kelly McClymer
All rights reserved, including the right of reproduction in whole or in part in any form.
SIMON PULSE and colophon are registered trademarks of Simon & Schuster, Inc.
Designed by Ann Zeak
The text of this book was set in Garamond 3.
Manufactured in the United States of America
First Simon Pulse edition March 2006
10 9 8 7 6 5 4 3 2
Library of Congress Control Number 2005936047
ISBN-13: 978-1-4169-1479-2
ISBN-10: 1-4169-1479-X

To Kristen, Andrew, and Brendan,
the three people who keep me young. Thank you.

Acknowledgments

This book wouldn't be the same book if it weren't for my excellent agent and advocate, Nadia Cornier, or the insights of my phenomenal editor, Michelle Nagler. I also want to thank my children for their patient answers to their mother's endless questions about growing up in the twenty-first century. Any inaccuracies are my own.

Getting to Third Date

One

Dear Mother Hubbard,
I think my bf has lost my cell number. We hung out every single second of last weekend and he said he'd call. I've skipped class all week (my professors make us turn our cell phones off in class), and he hasn't called yet. I'm thinking of slipping my number under his door. Do you think he would be embarrassed knowing I knew he lost my number?
Trying to Be Considerate

Dear Considerate,
Slip your number under his door?

Ummmm . . . not if you value your-self. Don't you get it? You've been dumped. Here's what you do: Go to the campus bookstore and slip a copy of *He's Just Not That Into You* into your backpack. There should be sev-eral copies, as I always have them restock when they run out. Read it. Twice if you need to. Then block his number on your cell and go back to class.

Mother Hubbard

I stepped closer to read what was scrawled over my column this week.

Mother Hubbard, Go Back to Your Cupboard.

In drippy red acrylic paint, someone—obviously a creatively and romantically tor-tured student from the Arts and Theater Department—has taken exception to my sensible advice, and this was her artistic way of telling me, or more precisely, Mother Hubbard, to take early retirement. Nice.

College. I thought it would be so dif-ferent from high school. Silly me. The

Mother Hubbard advice column nailed to the campus paper's office door and the big red slashed circle, universal sign of disdain, that covered it told me two things.

One, dating in college is just like dating in high school, with the exception that there are no parents to lie to or evade after an unfortunate curfew lapse.

Two, don't open the door to the *Campus Times.* I knew I should have turned around, fished my cell out of my pocket, and called Tyler, the paper's editor in chief, to claim a migraine. Or typhoid. Maybe Ebola. But I didn't.

For one thing, in the month I'd been writing the column Tyler had insisted I stay away from the paper's tiny basement office—he preferred to keep me very "Deep Throat." No one was supposed to know who Mother Hubbard was, and Tyler was determined not to be the first editor of the campus paper to let the secret slip. Not so easy in this age of teddy cams, picture phones, and instant messenger.

Maybe Tyler's overboard Secret Service/FBI clandestine meeting type of secrecy wasn't as overboard as I'd first thought when he'd asked (read "begged"—literally down on both knees) me to write the column.

What can I say? It was my first week on campus. I probably looked like easy prey. I was still under the naive impression that college was totally different from high school—after all, there was not a mom or dad in sight as I sat on my bed and he knelt on the floor in front of me, his head against my knee, begging me to take the column off his hands. How could I refuse? He pretended he was joking, but there was real desperation in his eyes. I'm a sucker for desperate.

Apparently the person who'd agreed to write it had switched both her major and her college over the summer, without giving him so much as a nanosecond's heads-up. He needed a columnist, and he needed her in time for the next day's paper. "The one everyone on campus reads," he boasted. As if that would make the job appealing.

He'd almost made the column sound cool—my advice read by millions . . . well, really twenty-five thousand; stepping into the shoes of those anonymous souls before me who had kept the secret of Mother Hubbard's identity without fail for a century.

But, if I have to be honest, it was the way his eyes turned from gold-brown to green-brown as he begged that got to me. I wanted some more time to study changeable eyes like that. Even David's had only been one color—a vibrant blue. Okay, let's not go there. David is history.

In my defense, I hadn't realized I was starting another one of those hopeless crushes that made my stomach hurt and my ears buzz as if my dad's electric razor were strapped on top of my head.

Not that Tyler was perfect. Nope.

For example, when I opened the door, offensive column in hand, it only took about two seconds for Tyler to look up and start gobbling. Yes. I do mean as in "Gobble-gobble-gobble." With appropriate elbow flapping to simulate a big bird. That's another thing I like about him. He's serious, with a sense of humor. Sometimes, however, that humor is seriously sick.

I wanted to laugh, but that would only encourage him and I was looking for a cure for the crush—and was determined not to let on that I was interested. I waved the torn-out column over my head. "That would be Mother Goose, not Mother Hubbard. Brush up on your nursery rhymes."

Clearly, he didn't care about his gross inaccuracy, because he continued to gobble. What else can you expect from someone who is seriously ambitious, but twisted enough to think he can make his mark on the campus paper by aiming more toward the audience of the *National Enquirer* than the *New York Times*? Like I said, college is really not as different from high school as it should be.

My parents had both told me that college would be hard, and that there would be adjustments to make. Foolish me, I'd been picturing adjustments like learning to say no to one guy when I already had a date scheduled with another. Juggling a social life and study sessions, keeping up with both. But no. I'd slipped right back into the high school role of best friend to my massive crush, who was too busy making goo-goo eyes at someone else to notice.

Comedy Central would pay for a stand-up routine of my first month in college.

So far, the only adjustments I'd had to make were finding an alarm clock loud enough to wake me now that my dad wasn't around to give his "third and final warning" bellow, and buying a pair of emergency jeans with a slightly larger waist for the days when I hit the dining hall ice cream cart a little too hard. Well, and learning to deal with being the most hated anonymous figure on campus, courtesy of the advice column I hadn't really wanted to write in the first place.

At least Tyler's teasing signaled it was okay to shed my deep cover—for the moment. The only two people in the office were Tyler and Sookie, his assistant editor and the one who refused to write the column at the last minute, even when he begged. Which meant that she was smarter than I was.

I slid over to Sookie's desk and slipped her lighter from her cigarettes. She already has a pack-a-day habit and a smoky voice that suggests throat cancer in the next thirty years. Whenever I see her,

I can't help thinking of Lois Lane, the no-nonsense, hardcore reporter whose only fault is that she can't tell that Clark Kent is really Superman.

Holding up the clipping of my (artistically vandalized) column, I put the lighter to it so the flame touched one torn corner. The paper began to char and smoke. Very satisfying.

Tyler stopped gobbling and leaped up. "You're going to set off the sprinklers." He grabbed the paper from my hand before it could burst into flame. Probably a good thing, considering the building (and its retrofitted sprinklers) were older than God. "You have to learn to take the criticism that comes with the job."

Sookie looked up from her laptop and nodded. "You should see what comes through campus mail for me." Sookie had the honor of putting together the campus police blotter for every other edition. No advice column for her; she's after the dirt on campus—which football player was found with an open beer, who pulled the fire alarm at midnight at the dorm. The police might not care, but Sookie did. Yep.

A real Lois Lane in the making. Well, with one difference. She didn't think she needed a man, never mind a Superman.

"Seen it." Courtesy of Tyler, who was probably one of the few people on earth who considered stalk-mail a compliment to his editorial acumen. The police blotter (not to mention the follow-up investigative report Sookie does) tends to bring out the worst in its subjects. She shrugged, not glancing up from her work. "At least you know it isn't personal—no one but you, Tyler, and I even know you're Mother Hubbard."

Tyler frowned and looked over his shoulder as if we were under surveillance. "I'd rather you didn't say that aloud."

Sookie slipped a cigarette between her lips as she considered his request. She didn't light it, because of the aforementioned overly sensitive sprinkler system, but she knew how much he hated her to have a cigarette, even if she didn't light it. "You'd *rather* a lot of things, Mr. Editor Man. But you can't have everything."

I could smell it in the air—the scent of an imminent fight. A common occurrence when two strong editorial egos collide. It was almost a tradition. Just like homecoming, graduation, and the one-hundred-year-old Mother Hubbard column, dispensing advice through the current unfortunate student minion. Like me.

I thought about saying something to diffuse the situation, but then I remembered how mad I was at Tyler for talking me into the stupid job in the first place.

"I thought you liked controversy, Tyler. Good for the bottom line." Bottom line: The more papers that were read, the more revenue the paper brought in from ad sales.

"I'd love the Mother Hubbard controversy, Katelyn—if it made people read the paper instead of burning it in front of the student union."

Sookie leaned forward. "Maybe I could do an investigation piece." Her eyes lit up, and I knew how some of her investigative targets must have felt. "That paper-burning stunt was cool! The firemen came, and the police. The local TV station loved it. They were interviewing students about whether or not the advice is horrible. Maybe I could spin this in our favor.

Freedom of speech is always good for some noise."

"It is media attention." Tyler perked up for just a minute. Then he slumped in his chair. "Of course, the TV anchors were laughing during the footage, right before they called the controversy 'student immaturity at work.' They didn't even get the name of the column right—they kept calling it Mommy Dearest. They were just interested in seeing a mob of girls in shorts and tank tops clapping and shouting 'Retire, Old Biddy!' as the paper burned."

Sookie, of course, taunted Tyler further, egged on by his desperation. "Maybe I could call my piece 'Retirement Time for Old Mother Hubbard?'"

Tyler barely reacted. He was prone to giving frantic, pompous "nose to the grindstone" speeches—not slumping in his chair like he was contemplating the end of his career before it even got started. But then, he was a junior—the first junior to be editor in chief since World War II.

I was so focused on enjoying his torment that it took a minute for me to digest what Sookie had just suggested. Retiring

Mother Hubbard. Oh, right. That's what I wanted!

Except . . . then what excuse would I have to talk to Tyler? We had one class together, so I could ask for notes, but since we both already knew I was the better note taker, it would make my interest in him pretty obvious. Hiding my feelings for guys who weren't feeling me was something I'd learned how to do flawlessly in high school. There probably wasn't a single person there who knew that I spent four years wishing David Morse would stop calling me his best friend. I hid it well. Unless you counted every best-friend-turned-lover song I had stored on my iPod.

I wanted to keep my flawless record intact.

Fortunately, Tyler didn't like the idea of retiring the oldest campus tradition (next to blowout parties, on Tuesdays, of all nights) any more than I did. "Forget it. We're not breaking tradition on my watch."

Not for the first time, I was glad Tyler had a teensy streak of pompous patriarchal idiot (I learned in high school a girl can't help whom she crushes on; it just happens, like tornados or zits). Until he continued, "Katelyn, you're going to have to give the people what they want. And fast."

"You mean instead of giving good advice, I should just tell them to go at it like mindless rabbits? No way."

I didn't like his solution, although I'd heard it before. Too many times. Readers thought I was too old-fashioned. That my dating rules were strict, and my tell-it-like-it-is tone way too harsh for a mother figure from a nursery rhyme.

But I disagree. The one benefit of writing the column was that I could use the common sense I'd learned watching all the high school drama around me. Love is blind, deaf, and dumb, and if I had to write about it, the least I could do was try to help some of the hapless victims of pheromone overload see their way to avoiding a few Mr. or Miss No-Nos. For example, it's one thing to have a crush, but entirely another to make a fool of yourself in front of said crush—whether he notices or not.

I think Tyler and I were both surprised that I'd actually said no to his suggestion

—okay, really it was a demand. "Why is it so hard for you to be reasonable?" He spun aimlessly in his beat-up chair, a sign he was taking this whole thing a lot more seriously than I'd realized. "College is for learning about relationships and stuff like that."

For a second I thought about caving and letting him off the hook. But there's a reason why my parents tell me I'd make a good lawyer. I'm stubborn when I think I'm right. I smiled at Tyler and said smugly, "Key word: 'learning.' Not 'wallowing.'"

"People already feel bad enough getting dumped, they don't need you to rub it in." Tyler got so mad his little tic started showing. I liked that tic, usually.

It was a blue vein that swelled and pulsed right at the left curve of his temple. Reminded me of the heroes in some of the romance novels I used to sneak out of my mother's room when I was twelve. They had a tic when they got mad too.

I liked knowing that I could make Tyler really mad. After all, the best defense is a good offense, my high school swimming coach used to say. But this time I worried a little that the tic was going to blow.

I thought I'd lighten the mood. A little. "Why can't people party without breaking hearts?"

Oops. Apparently, that came out a tad too serious to be funny. I brushed my hair behind my ear and felt my cheeks flushing red. Tyler stared at me. "You have to fix this. You're *ruining* me."

"You? Not the paper?" Which was a joke, of course.

The *Campus Times* was in no risk of ruin. In fact, it had been in constant circulation since 1906. How do I know such a thing? It was my misfortune to be drafted to search the microfiche archives to find fun or scandalous facts about the newspaper for its hundredth anniversary. (What can I say? He needed it quickly, and like I said, a girl can't help who turns her to semi-mindless mush.)

My jab hit home because Tyler turned white. But he regrouped quickly. "I meant the paper, of course, but I am the paper— I'm the editor." I guess that was a good sign for his future ambitions—he could give anything a positive spin and polish.

Sookie broke the tension between us by laughing. "The seventy-fifth editor, to be precise. And the paper has survived seventy-four editors, some of them worse than you." Lois Lane to the rescue.

Only not. Because Tyler said, without looking at me, "I thought we agreed to make this paper great? We were just starting to get taken seriously." Read, the paper was getting some decent ad money from the beer companies and local liquor stores. "I think Katelyn may have found a way to destroy the paper and our good work . . . or at least the integrity and longevity of Mother Hubbard."

TWO

Whoa. That was a bit harsh. We were just talking about a silly advice column—no one took it seriously, did they? Even the burning was probably what the TV news said—students blowing off steam for a little attention. Wasn't it? It was my turn to regroup. Fortunately, I'm as good (maybe better) at it than Tyler. "Well, that's what they fail to pay you the big bucks for. You're the editor. Sookie's right: You figure out how to take advantage of the controversy. Let her do an investigative piece. Leave me out of it. I stand by my advice."

"Oh yeah? Well maybe we should run your face instead of Mother Hubbard's tomorrow. Maybe then you wouldn't have such an easy time telling people they're wasting their time."

"What's so wrong with telling people to use common sense instead of wishful thinking? Facts are facts. The guy—or girl—who is borrowing notes is not Prince or Princess Charming. They just want to pass the class, not make a pass."

Sookie sighed. "Spoken like an engineering major. What other kind of advice besides practical did you expect her to give, Tyler?"

"Good advice." He frowned at Sookie and me.

As for me, I didn't like the way Sookie made "engineering" sound like a four-letter word. But before I could say anything, Tyler's rampage continued.

"How would you like everyone knowing you were the one giving the twisted conservative advice that didn't even work back in the fifties?"

I'd hate it. Fortunately, so would he. We both knew it was an empty threat, and I didn't give him the satisfaction of a direct answer. I held out my JumpDrive stiffly.

"Can you just download my column so I can go home and go to bed?"

"Fine." He plugged in the drive and downloaded my column. I held my breath while he handed me back my JumpDrive. I was almost out of the office before he read the column I'd just written. The one where I'd suggested that Miss Treated should swear off guys until the semester was over and she'd passed all her subjects.

His wolf howl stopped me cold. "You have to do the column over, Katelyn. I can't put this one out. We'll get bombed!"

I countered, almost hoping he'd fire me from the job I hadn't wanted in the first place. But not quite. "I'm right. *That's* what they don't like."

"You're telling this girl that the guys she's going out with are just using her."

"Aren't they?" I ticked off the reasons Miss Treated had sent in her letter. "One, they borrow her notes and don't return them. Two, they say they'll call and they never do until right before a test. Three, when she stalks them down, they run in the opposite direction to avoid her."

He couldn't really argue. Miss Treated

was really Miss Doormat. He shrugged and mumbled, "Well, girls do the same thing."

Oops. I had stepped too hard on Tyler's weakness. Sophia. My roommate. His unfortunate crush. Not that he hid it well.

He was smitten with her, from her sassy black hair to her cute Italian accent. I knew about Tyler's crush because I knew all about how people who are dying to hide their crush find ways to be with the person without letting the secret slip. For example, Tyler usually collected my column directly from my room—when he knew Sophia would be around. I really hate talking to a guy who is sneaking glances at someone else.

I think we all knew (well, except for Tyler, maybe) he could "discuss" journalism with Sophia forever and it wasn't going to go further than that. . . . But somehow he thought she would eventually succumb to his editorial wiles. Yeah, right.

So while he was right, in principle, that many girls treated guys just as badly as guys treated girls, I thought it best to head off that conversation. "I don't. I let the guy know if it isn't working for me. I have zero game-playing tolerance."

"That's right. You always turn down guys for a third date if they don't rate high by the second date. *So* nineteen-fifties." He shook his head at me, as if I were a two-year-old who had just stuck my finger in a light socket. "I'm more real than that. I don't need a stupid rating system, I listen to what's in here." He thumped his chest.

I was a little surprised he had remembered. I'd rambled about it one night when I'd had too much coffee and too many letters from students who seemed to cling to people whom I wouldn't have given one date, never mind a third.

Stupid rating system? For a guy who thought he was so different, Tyler certainly seemed to think like everyone else on campus. "Whatever. I don't know how I'll survive with my four-point GPA."

Sookie laughed. "Give me a hot story over a hot guy—or an A— any day."

"Whatever." Tyler ran his hands through his hair. He looked like the Thinker with ADD. Apparently, having his hair stand on end helped his process. "Never mind. I'll rewrite it."

"Whatever." I pretended I didn't care. I

didn't want to care. The column was stupid. The questions were stupid. But I was used to succeeding at what I did. At least at assignments and tasks. I never failed. Especially not in such a spectacularly public (if anonymous) fashion.

And I knew too, firsthand, that just because Tyler might hang around Sophia it didn't mean he'd ever speak to me again if I didn't come through for him with this column. I was only a good *friend,* after all. Love really sucks sometimes.

Tyler probably would have rewritten my column, complete with advice to keep the student body trapped in relationships that would only make them miserable, if not for one little thing. More precisely, my little black book (okay, it was pink), which fell out of my purse as I opened it to jam in the JumpDrive. The little pink book in question, the one that held my thoughts on all the guys I'd ever gone out with. Or had considered going out with in the future.

I didn't even have a second to scoop it safely back inside my purse before Tyler snatched it up. "Let me just see this little rating system of yours, then, if it's so great."

"Hey. You won't understand it. It's in code. Give it back."

He carried my book over to Sookie's desk, and the two of them bent over it, murmuring, "Numbers . . . Just like an engineer . . . Oooh, who's this? . . . Milk Dud Breath?" while I threw erasers at them (the office had a ton, left over from the pre-computer era) and demanded they return my private property. I wasn't too worried that they'd crack my code. But still. The book contained nicknames, stats, bits of information, and columns to check whether or not the guy was . . .

Tyler caught one of the erasers and threw it back. It bounced off my desk and landed in the trash. "What does TDW mean?"

"Third-Date Worthy." I could have (should have) refused to explain.

"Not just date worthy?" Sookie seemed nonplussed at the idea that I'd judge a man in the same way she rated the newsworthiness of the story leads she chased down in the police blotter every week.

Not for me, though. "If they're not even date worthy, I don't list them."

"Then how do you remember who you've already ruled out?"

Just how many guys did she think I knew? Forget that, I don't want to know.

"I have a good memory." I wasn't going to put my record of one date a week up against the record of someone like Sophia's of one date for breakfast, one for lunch, and one for dinner.

"This is the key to Katelyn—to Mother Hubbard." Tyler held the book up like it was the Holy Grail, or a Pulitzer, which, after one beer too many and a broken-hearted night with Sophia's paying zippo attention to him, he'd confessed he coveted winning one day. He hadn't seemed to make the connection that scandal didn't usually win prizes. Except maybe Deep Throat and Watergate. But that was before celebrity sex videos hit the Internet and changed the scandal scales big-time.

He thumbed through the book. "What do the codes mean? RTG1-2."

"Nothing."

Sookie whistled low in her throat— approvingly, I think. "Wow. You've got the blog address, and the online dating profile?" She looked up and grinned at me. "I'm surprised you don't have the blood type."

"That would come later," I snapped. "Can I have that back, please?"

Tyler grabbed it. "Man, you have more research on guys than Uncle Sam." His happiness was unsettling. And then a shadow crossed his face. "Anything on me?"

That was *all* I needed him to see. "No. Only guys I might date. Could you give it back, please? You two have work to do, and we don't want anyone to notice how long I've been in here, do we?"

For a moment Tyler held on to the book as if he wanted to go through it to make sure I was telling the truth. Not a good idea. I considered whether my six weeks of karate back in sixth grade would be enough to take him down. Maybe. If he was unconscious.

Fortunately, in typical clueless guy fashion, he only seemed relieved that I didn't consider him in the slightest bit date worthy.

He handed me the book. "This rating

system of yours would make a great column."

"No, thank you!"

"Why not?" He seemed surprised that I wouldn't immediately agree. "It works for you, right?"

"Of course." Sure, if you want a catalog of losers, but I wasn't going to go there. Especially not with Tyler.

"Maybe if the readers know why you're so sure that giving up early is a good thing, they'll stop sending you trash mail, right?"

"Yes." I wasn't sure I liked where this was going. After all, my rating system was for my eyes only. Top secret. Hush-hush. Not to mention highly embarrassing.

He got that ADD Thinker look again. "Let me get the paper to bed and then I'll figure out where to go from here."

"You could always just fire me."

"That would be the traditional response." He grinned at me and my auto no turned into a definite maybe. Serious guys with a surprise sense of humor. I'm just a sucker for that combination. "And I'm anything but traditional. I'll think of something."

"Great." I didn't even bother to fake enthusiasm as I escaped from the office (after Tyler checked to make sure no one suspicious was loitering outside). I was going to be doing some thinking too. About how to stop my hormones from dancing a little salsa whenever Tyler was in sight.

There are times when I resent that college kids—especially freshmen—often get stuck in classes of hundreds. Like cattle. What do they think? So many of us will fail that it isn't worth wasting a few more teachers on us? Maybe that we'll be so happy for the new freedom of college life, we'll be impressed by a teacher who is so far away she's teaching from another zip code? Oh, well. What is, is.

Look for the silver lining—which is, I guess, besides the fact that my school has a great mic system in the auditoriums, that I can sit very far away from Tyler and not have to hear whatever insane plans he's come up with during his all-nighter putting the paper to bed, aided no doubt by a gallon of Starbucks' finest.

I took a seat far away from my usual row in the auditorium and crouched down low so that Tyler wouldn't see me in a casual scan of the room. I don't know what it is about me. But I really don't know how to give up hope with a guy. Anything else, sure. But that a guy might suddenly notice me as more than a friend? Nope. I can crush it, burn it, starve it, and stomp it, but the hope always sneaks up when I least expect it.

Like when Tyler came into the room just then in jeans that were a little too tight and a green sweatshirt that made the green flecks in his hazel eyes stand out. He stopped, noticed that I was not in our usual row. I hoped he'd just take his seat, but no such luck. He wandered around long enough to spot me, and then slid into the seat next to me. So why was I glad he was there, when I purposely tried to avoid him? Please, don't try to force me to make sense of something that human beings haven't figured out in many millennia.

He didn't even know he'd insulted me the night before—or that I knew he was really taking advantage of my crush on him. Although, maybe he *didn't* know how I felt. Maybe he's just thick and self-absorbed. Oops, there goes that little note of hope growing again. Because if he were just self-absorbed, there would still be the possibility that he might notice me as more than good old Katelyn. Then maybe his hormones would want to dance with my hormones. . . . What can I say, I'm hopeless.

Almost as if he knew what I was thinking, Tyler said, "So—ready to learn how to French-kiss?" Which was a funny commentary on the syllabus entry for today, or a cruel torture meme, depending on whether or not he had a clue how I feel.

"I know how to French-kiss." At least, I've never had any complaints, but I didn't need to add that aloud.

"Yeah, I hope Golding plans to explain why she thinks she needs to spend a whole class on kissing. Unless she's going to have us practice."

I bet half the class took Human Sexuality, not just because it fulfilled a general credit to graduate and was thought—erroneously—to be an easy-A class, but because we were naive enough to think it might be a shortcut to solving the mysteries of attraction, love, and heartbreak. Maybe give us an academic defense to guard against broken hearts, against loving someone who wouldn't love us back. Or, at the least, a way to weed out the duds before we did something stupid, like lend them our last twenty bucks.

Class was full to the brim with plenty of young, confused, dating-eligible students— not all freshmen, I might point out. There were some upperclassmen, like Tyler and Sophia, who often have better things to do than go to class, if you know what I mean. Although, I think Sophia just liked to have her expertise in the subject confirmed. If that sounds a little bitchy, it isn't. Sophia's totally cool and doesn't even seem to mind, too much, that she got stuck with a tomboyishly cute freshman for a roommate.

I almost didn't even mind that Tyler had the hots for her. I'd gotten used to being second-string in high school, and once again college wasn't much different. Besides, who can compete with a girl from

Italy with excellent taste in fashion and room decor? It was a no-brainer that she'd take Human Sexuality just for the easy A.

I wonder how many other people in the class were relieved to hear, the very first class, that it wasn't our shallowness that made it difficult to return the affections of someone deserving. It was just basic chemistry. Our bodies made the decision from a few short sniffs and a little visual selectivity.

For example, my obsession with Tyler's eyes. Not to mention the way he smelled like peppermint and leather. And Richie's bizarre thing for my ear. How do I know that? Because he told me. He even wrote an ode to my ear for a dramatic performance once. He gave me a private showing and I applauded, even though it creeped me out a little.

I mean, my ear? Why not my smile? Or my eyes? Heck, even my legs, which are a trigger for male fantasies, according to my professor. But I guess we're just slaves to our own chemistry.

There was a ray of hope on the attraction

front, though. Professor Golding says it eases up as we get older. Probably because we start losing our sense of smell. And our eyesight becomes fuzzier. But I'm only eighteen, and I'm not anxious to get old before I've been young. So I guess I'm just going to have to put up with the vagaries of pheromones. And the fact that my pheromones enjoy leading me into unrequited like with guys whose pheromones don't reciprocate.

Tragedy in the making, I say. But my body chemistry obviously didn't consult my wishes. If it had, I'd have gone out with David in high school. Or, at the very least, Tyler would have noticed me in the boy meets girl way during the past few weeks.

I tried not to let it get to me, although I had added to the end of my last essay, on the subject of human hormones, the rather impulsive and off-topic sentence: *I wish I controlled my body chemistry rather than it controlling me.*

Professor Golding had written a note alongside my lament: *Ah! But the uncertainty is what makes it all exciting!*

She could afford to say that—she was

already at the stage where her sense of smell and her eyesight were going.

Mine, however, were still pretty sharp. And Tyler was a cutie, even though I was trying not to look at him. There was no discussion of Mother Hubbard at all from him, which threw me for a second. But then I noticed how he kept glancing at the empty seat next to me. Duh. He wasn't being his usual overcautious self. He had something other than the paper on his mind this morning.

"Where's Sophia?" His question reminded me that sometimes a sexy roommate can come in handy (not usually, but sometimes). At the same time I had to fight the red tide of jealousy. Damned pheremones.

Sometimes I wish I wasn't so good at guessing what people will say—at least the things I wish they wouldn't say. Not that Tyler isn't nonchalant enough to fool anyone sitting nearby.

So I tell him only half the truth. "She wasn't feeling well, so I promised to take great notes and fill her in when I get back to the room." No need for him to know that the cause of Sophia's "illness" is six feet, six inches tall and a huge fan of some sports tournament at the bar. Sophia hadn't said good-bye to him until four in the morning—and I had cause to know since I was propped up on the lumpy, spine killer couch in the commons area of our dormitory until she gave me the all clear.

Okay, so there's one more adjustment I had to make to college life versus high school life. Sharing a room. I'm not an only child, but my little brother and I always had our own rooms. Sharing with someone who is yin to my yang is way weird.

Not that Tyler would get it—he's dying to yin her yang. Guys.

Golding walked into class with a massive pair of lips resting on her shoulders. At least, I assumed it was Golding, since the body beneath the lips was the same curvy yet conservatively clad figure that had somehow made the guys drool all semester.

She liked to shock us, always laughing when she got the silent hush at the sheer daring of her latest stunt. Then she'd smile a big Cheshire Cat grin and say, "It comes with the material. Can you believe they pay me to teach you guys about sex and love?"

But giant plastic lips in place of a head was a bit much. In my opinion. Tyler seemed to think it was cool, the way he was smiling. I suppose any diversion is a good diversion when you need one.

Some of the other kids clapped. Not too surprising when you think about it—a class of hundreds is bound to have a small percentage of people who like their humor on the cute but cheesy side.

Golding's hottie grad student assistant helped her get the lips off of her head and onto the little lecture desk at the front of the classroom. Her hair was a little mussed, but not much—she patted it absently as she faced the class, and adjusted her glasses as she peered up at the faces in the crowded lecture hall.

That was something I really did like about Professor Golding—she came by her sex appeal naturally. She wore minimal makeup and her clothes were the right size, not too tight. She had a killer sense of humor and such complete comfort in her own skin that there wasn't any way not to love her—even when she had a pair of giant lips on her head.

Even when she was outrageous. "Raise your hand if you think you're a good kisser."

Lots of people raised their hands—Tyler's may even have been the first one up, he responded so quickly. Maybe he thought she'd ask him to come up and demonstrate. Hey, if my hope dies hard, I can imagine that holds true for other people, even guys like Tyler.

"No wonder no one takes your advice," Tyler whispered when I didn't raise my hand.

"This is a bogus question." I crossed my arms to avoid the temptation to raise my hand. I noticed a few hands that hadn't been up raise waveringly—no one really likes to be in the minority. Including me.

But I wasn't going to give Golding's lame question any validity.

I'd forgotten that Tyler could lose his sense of humor and revert back to serious in about a tenth of a second. "I am a good kisser. Are you implying I'm not?"

As if I'd know. Maybe once or twice (an

hour) I've thought about it. Tyler has great lips, full and curved and quirked just like I like them.

Of course, I'd fall on the sharpest pencil I could find before I'd admit that to him. So I just said, "Everybody thinks they're a great kisser—it's the other person they think doesn't know jack."

He grinned, sense of humor resurfacing, as if he thought I'd agreed with him. But no, he'd heard me. "Go ahead and keep telling yourself that."

Golding's lecture was pretty much what I'd expected (after all, I had read the chapter she'd assigned us to read—maybe I do like being in the minority, after all). A quick historical overview, some of the more weirdo views that cultures hold on kissing, how kissing can go horribly wrong, etc.

To Tyler's (and probably others') disappointment, there was no practicing. Even Professor Golding restricted herself to kissing the obscenely huge lips only five times, and she didn't French-kiss even once, although several people anonymously—and loudly—called out for it.

We had pretty much exhausted the

topic, except for jokes, a good ten minutes before class was finished. I was hoping for an early exit, but unfortunately, one of the adoring throng had a question unrelated to the topic of kissing—but very related to me and my life.

"Do you think Mother Hubbard has gone senile and should retire?"

Three

Professor Golding doesn't usually get mad about anything. So I was shocked to see her actually turn red and shake her finger at us—the collective us, since she didn't have a clue who was Mother Hubbard either. Thank goodness, as it turns out.

Because, while I was anonymous, Tyler wasn't. And she turned her eyes to the editor of the paper. "Did you ask Dr. Laura to write the Mother Hubbard column this year, Tyler?"

"Oooooooooh." The class knew that was a burn of the highest magnitude. Professor Golding hated Dr. Laura, the iconic and intolerant talk radio host.

Even though most of us didn't listen to her radio program, we know a lot about her attitudes: adoption over abortion, single parents don't date until children leave home, wives coddle their poor "less capable" husbands to keep their marriages happy, and—worst of all to Professor Golding, who had three children and a full-time job—mothers stay home with their children, no excuses, no escape.

Tyler, the freak, preened under her glare. "Her fee was too high, so I had to settle for a freshman who wanted to set her fellow students straight."

Thanks, Tyler, tell everyone Mother Hubbard is a freshman. That quarters the possible candidates. Normally, I wouldn't care, but when people are burning your column in the streets, you start to realize you have to be a little bit careful. Or at least, you do if you're not Tyler, the normally-paranoid-turned-suddenly-clueless-by-the-spotlight editor.

That clue he'd inadvertently dropped obviously did not escape Professor Golding. "A freshman? Clearly, a very inexperienced freshman. Perhaps you would have been wiser to give the job to someone who had learned that no person—or relationship—is perfect."

Tyler nodded, but I could feel the ego rising off him as he stood to address the crowd, not just Professor Golding. "Is there something wrong with not settling?"

I turned alternately hot and then cold. He was using my lines against me, when he hadn't believed a word I'd said. He had to be doing it to irritate Professor Golding. Or me. Or, more likely, both of us. Still, I admit I felt pleased that he'd remembered what I'd said well enough to quote me.

It was a toss-up which of us wanted him to sit down and shut up more. But since it was Professor Golding's class—and I was being discreet—she took the first shot. "I am the last person to suggest that anyone 'settle,' as you say, Tyler. But I don't like how quickly Mother Hubbard advises someone to write off another human being."

"Here's how it was explained to me," Tyler said innocently, leaning forward earnestly for maximum effect. "Mother Hubbard thinks that you date a person once, and you are going to be almost certain whether they meet your standards or not. But, regardless, everybody deserves a second chance. After that—third dates only go to a chosen few."

Professor Golding pushed her glasses farther up her nose—a signal to those of us who had been in her lectures that she was preparing to engage in verbal battle. But all she said, rather mildly, was, "That isn't an awful premise."

I was warmed for a moment by Professor Golding's faint praise of my philosophy. Silly me. Because her voice had a little edge when she added, "However, Mother Hubbard appears to have set such high standards that only saints and robots could meet them on the first date."

"Yeah," one beefy football type called out. "My girlfriend dumped me because of a Mother Hubbard column. I didn't do nothin' to deserve it."

Unfortunately for him, his pity party was cut short. He hadn't remembered that said girlfriend also took the class. She rose from a seat on the other side of the room and pointed at him. "Joe Jackmeyer, there's nothing wrong with Mother Hubbard saying that if you only came over for booty calls and never let anyone see us in public that I was wasting my time with you."

The tough football guy fell apart, as if this was the first time he'd heard the accusation—untrue, since clearly he had read my column. "Baby. If you'd only talked to me about it. . . . I'll take you out in public."

"You will?" She seemed skeptical, but I saw it—hope was rising faster than she could stop it. She wanted to believe him.

"Sure. I just didn't want to share you." What a line.

Line or not, it worked. The girl would have flown over the turning heads if she could. "Okay."

I didn't believe him. But the girlfriend who formerly had been only a booty call clearly did. I wondered what she'd be writing to Mother Hubbard in the future? I'd give the new "public" romance a good two weeks . . . if they were lucky.

"See?" Professor Golding obviously didn't see the same thing I did. She was practically beaming. "That's what's needed—a little more communication, a little more compassion, and a healthy dose of tolerance."

The class echoed her last statement. We'd heard it many times during the semester. It was Professor Golding's battle cry, after all.

I wanted to do something really stupid —like argue with Professor Golding. She was actually the kind of professor who'd give you extra credit for arguing with her. But my defending Mother Hubbard, being a freshman, and sitting next to Tyler was just too many clues to drop when Mother Hubbard hatred was spreading across campus.

Besides, Professor Golding was not yet done. "Perhaps you should consider replacing your columnist, Tyler."

"How's this . . ." Oh, God. I'd been so focused on the professor that I'd forgotten Tyler and his vow to come up with a solution to his editorial dilemma regarding the Mother Hubbard column. He had the gleam in his eye that meant he was getting an idea. This was a dangerous look. But I couldn't think of a way to shut him up, short of screaming "Fire!" And the dorm RA—our unofficial campus mommy, yet one more difference between college and home—had warned us more than once that ever since 9/11 the campus administrators had become very intolerant of false alarms.

"What?" Professor Golding stood with her hands on her hips, challenging him.

"Well." He smiled that smile that had won him quite a bit of advertising for the paper. The one that had triggered my crush. The one I was rapidly coming to hate more than pop quizzes. "Why don't I ask Mother Hubbard to reconsider three of her own rejects for third date?"

Professor Golding pushed up her glasses. "You mean, give them each a chance for a third date before she makes up her mind?"

Tyler smiled more widely. "Exactly!"

Maybe, despite the fact that Sophia was clearly immune, Tyler's smile got to more people than silly little Katelyn, because Professor Golding did not smush him with a few well-placed verbs. Instead, she nodded. "I like it."

I didn't. But that probably goes without saying.

Tyler bowed, as if he'd done the professor a courtly service. "Expect a report in next Thursday's issue on which guy Mother Hubbard's going to give another chance." He grinned. "We'll save the recap for next week, to give her the weekend."

"I'm impressed with your open mind, Tyler." Professor Golding was practically beaming at him. Everyone else had a puzzled look, like they didn't quite know what to think—was Mother Hubbard now good, or was she bad?

I could have told them. Mother Hubbard was mightily pissed and ready to strangle the current editor of the *Campus Times*. Not that he knew it. Or would have cared even if he did.

When the class began to clap, after deciding Mother Hubbard was taking the right step in giving a guy another chance, and Tyler made another bow, it took all my will not to put my hand on his tight blue-jeaned butt and push.

It was there, in my face, as he stood happily lapping up the applause and praise.

He hadn't even asked me if I'd do it. I was now stuck in a worse predicament than I had been in before. Tyler taking a tumble down the tiered seats seemed like the only way to fix the horrible mess he had just handed me.

"I'm glad to see you're going to try to gently guide Mother Hubbard to a more tolerant column, Tyler. Let's hope she learns quickly."

I glanced at the worn jeans Tyler wore. His campus ID was hanging out, attached to the keys stuffed in his pocket, the little square photo smiling at me. One push. That's all it would take. Preferably a tumble all the way to the bottom where he could take out Professor Golding like a bowling ball takes out a lone tenpin.

Four

"Just tell him to forget it."

Sophia doled out her ruthless advice between applying hot pink lipstick and dabbing concealer on the slightly bluish semicircles under her eyes. Otherwise, of course, she looked fabulous for someone who'd been up until 4 a.m.

"Easy for you to say. You pass up one good thing and you know another will be coming along. Like tonight. Is it Jake or Tom?"

"Jake." She smiled. "We're going to the private room at his club." Jake was not a student, he was a twentysomething who'd decided his future lay in selling drinks and booking hot new bands to entice students to his club. He liked to say (in fact, it was on his marquee) that he'd earned his degree in success one tequila at a time. "Want to come along?"

"No, thanks. I'm not into the club scene." At least, I didn't think I would be, so I'd avoided it.

"One day you're going to have to take a chance or two, Katelyn." I'd noticed life was unfair in high school, but living with Sophia underscored that nasty little truth big-time. She was beautiful, sexy, smart, and a good roommate, too. I'd kept waiting for the big nasty secret about this seemingly perfect person to surface. No dice.

Along with all her other stellar traits, Sophia was a very good listener. Maybe too good, since she had just blasted through all my pretense about why I was writing the column in the first place. I had added her to the list of those select few who knew my secret identity early on. I needed someone to vent to. Unfortunately, she was apparently of the same mind as all the other students on campus.

I know, it was risky of me to confess my

secret to Sophia when I barely knew her. But in my defense, I think a little of Tyler's paranoid caution had rubbed off, because I didn't tell her until she had pinky sworn not to tell anyone (including Tyler), after I explained the concept of pinky swearing to her and she'd gotten her amusement at the idea out of her system.

"What about how I took a chance on being Mother Hubbard?" I defended myself, while wondering how the gold-brown eye shadow she was brushing on her eyelids would look on me. Which was another annoyingly perfect thing about Sophia. She was generous to a fault. Instead of revealing some secret ugly side, she'd helped me straighten out my eyebrows so that I wasn't unibrow city, and my makeup so that I added some flattering colors to my previously blue and green high school palette.

"An anonymous old crab who tells other people what to do about their lives because she doesn't have the desire to put her own heart on the line?" She shook her mascara wand at me in mock reproof. "You are too young for that."

"I—"

She stopped my weak protest with one final wave of the wand before stowing it away in its leather case. I had yet to discover where she bought her makeup. Maybe in Italy.

She looked at me seriously. "Sometimes I wonder if you only chose to write this column because you want to get closer to Tyler."

"Don't be silly. He's not interested in me."

I waited for her to protest (hope springs eternal—and painful) but she just nodded. "His interest in you has nothing to do with your interest in him. And I am worried that you have found no one interesting since you have been on campus."

That was unfair. "It's only been six weeks! I've gone out with the frat guy and the guy I met in the student loan line at the bursar's office too."

"One boy here, one boy there. And always some reason why you don't want to go out with them after the second time. Are you sure it is not because you are waiting for Tyler to notice you?" She looked hard at me.

I shook my head. I'm not great at lying, but she would have needed more than a hot curling iron to get that particular truth from me.

"Good." She nodded, and I breathed a sigh of relief that she had believed me. Until she stood up, shook out her hair, and said, "Because if you decide you want him, you shouldn't waste one more minute writing this silly column, you should ask him out directly."

"Mother Hubbard doesn't believe in girls asking boys out."

"Mother Hubbard is a cranky hundred-year-old. You're eighteen. Wouldn't you like to take a chance and go after what you want?"

I wasn't so sure. "Maybe it wouldn't be so bad to go back to the way they used to do it. Like on TV sitcoms. You know. The guy rings the doorbell, the father scares him silly, and the couple goes out on a real, official 'date.'"

"What a waste of time."

"I wouldn't call a clear signal of interest a waste. I'm tired of wasting time trying to figure out if someone likes me or just doesn't have anything better to do than hang out or 'grab coffee' with me. I think Mother Hubbard is right to advocate a little old-fashioned practicality."

Sophia made a *tch* noise with her tongue and teeth. "Mother Hubbard needs to find a good man. And you need to stop wasting time writing this silly column just so you can hang out with Tyler. Why don't you tell Tyler you quit? Then ask him if he wants to hang out. You'll know whether he's interested quick enough without Mother Hubbard to confuse things."

Clearly, however, she had not fully grasped the point of all my previous whining if she was going to suggest I quit. So I tried to explain it to her. "But I agreed to do the stupid column. I'm a person of my word."

She looked at me skeptically.

"I'm a woman of my word." I continued to defend my utterly foolish refusal to quit. "Besides, I'm right."

Sophia wrinkled her nose at me, a gesture I had come to accept as her European sign language for *don't be an idiot*. "Do you want to be right, or do you want to be happy?"

Well, to be honest, I wanted to take that fabulous Italian concealer peeking up out of her makeup case and rub it all over her beautiful face. I hate that question, which has been adopted by everyone on campus.

"Don't worry. Be happy." Pop psychology at its most mindless. It helps sum up Professor Golding's simplistic philosophy about love and relationships—and it explains why everyone hates Mother Hubbard's plainspoken (and correct) advice. Not that I'm biased or anything.

"I'd rather someone notice I'm right. That would make me happy."

"You always think with your brain, Katelyn, that's your problem." Quintessential Sophia. She shrugged, dabbed a bit of lipstick off her teeth, and smiled at herself in her mirror.

Perhaps I should have been more polite to the someone who knew I was the power behind the hated keyboard of Mother Hubbard. But I was still steaming from class. "Thanks. I guess I should be like you and think with something south of the border."

"South of the border?" It took her a minute to translate the idiom, but she'd been on campus for three years now, so she eventually got it. She shook her head. "You Americans are so provincial."

"Tell that to Candy. She was born in Iowa and never left the state until she came here to college." If Sophia was the gourmet taster of all things guy, Candy could be considered the poster child for the less-than-choosy girl. There was a pool going in the dorm for the date when Candy would leave school because (a) she was pregnant, or (b) she had a communicable disease so horrible she needed to be quarantined.

Sophia shuddered very delicately. If there'd been a guy in the room, he'd have reached for his jacket without thinking about it. "There are Candys in Italy, too, Katelyn. There are Candys everywhere. But just because someone stuffs herself with bad food does not mean others who are more sensible shouldn't enjoy a fine meal. Just so with sex."

She had a point. But I didn't have to let her know that. "Most guys can't tell the difference when it comes to sex."

Sophia tinkled, a bell-like laugh that was highly irritating unless you happened to have testosterone to spare. For just a minute I considered changing roommates at Christmas break. "Ah well, some guys *are* less than particular when it comes to sex. It is up to women to teach them better."

"Well, Candy isn't getting much of a chance to teach anyone anything with the revolving door she's got going. Besides, I'm not talking about sex, I'm talking about relationships. What makes two people click, and stay clicked?" It occurred to me that I had lived with Sophia for six weeks already. I should know better than to think the conversation would not, somehow, get steered back to sex.

"Why be so serious so soon?" Sophia seemed truly perplexed. "We are young. It is our time to have fun."

Yeah. Right. Some people had claimed that about high school, too. But after being in a high school class of eighty—most of us had been together since kindergarten—I had looked forward to the chance to find a wider guy pool in college.

Although the pool was definitely bigger here, so far the guys weren't much different from those in high school. In fact, to me, it seemed like a bigger pool just meant more confusion. I couldn't help longing for the good old days when a date wasn't called "hanging out." When words like "boyfriend" and "girlfriend" had established rules and didn't just pop out by surprise after some unspecified time when hanging out turned into habit.

There weren't many people on campus who shared my antiquated opinion, though—including Sophia, obviously. Was Tyler insane? To think that Mother Hubbard's espousing the Third-Date Theory would turn the readership from rage to worship? Or was he setting me up for more controversy, to get the paper a little more notice?

Speak of the devil. The triple rap on the door was distinctive. Tyler. No doubt he was going to make sure I'd do the column. After all, I'd left class as soon as it ended, without another word to him.

On the other hand, he could just be after his daily Sophia fix, since she'd missed class.

We were on the third floor, but I still reflexively looked out the window. Jumping was not an option. "Don't answer it. Maybe he'll—"

The door opened. Sophia never locked it; she didn't believe in locks, not even after my laptop got jacked. I didn't know if it was a European thing, a feminist thing, or just a Sophia thing. Whatever it was, I was stuck with it as long as we were roommates, and I'd seen other girls have much worse roommate problems, so I wasn't complaining.

Tyler walked in with his eyes closed. "Are you girls decent?"

Sophia's laugh tinkled. "No, but we *women* are dressed. Sorry to disappoint you, Tyler."

In the time I'd known her, I'd seen her put two dozen guys in their place, but always with that sexy smile that kept them from taking offense. Her papers in her gender studies classes could blister the paint off a men's only club (I proofread them for her since she still had a few English-as-a-second-language grammar blips). I guess the guys she dated didn't ask to read them.

Tyler was as full of himself as he had been in class. He practically strutted in the door, ignoring Sophia's delicate frown of displeasure. "So, have you figured out who your guinea pig will be?" He glanced at Sophia and I knew we were in for a covert ops verbal exchange while he tried to communicate about the column with me while keeping Sophia in the dark.

It would have been easier if he would just ask me to walk out in the quad with him—but that would mean leaving Sophia behind. Too bad for him I was just not up to secret agent subterfuge right then.

Sophia said nothing, but she looked at me with expectation. She believes women should regularly snap men on the nose with a rolled-up newspaper, as if they were errant puppies. Me? I've never been able to snap a puppy on the nose, even when said puppy has just filled a favorite shoe with a little treat.

However, it occurred to me I could irritate if not snap. So I said the one thing meant to drive Tyler over the edge of paranoia. "You don't need to be coy. Sophia knows."

Five

"You just tell him that?" Sophia looked shocked. "Why did you make me pinky swear, then?" She looked at her finger for a moment, as if it were damaged from our pinky-swearing moment. But then she shrugged, and I thought I saw a glimmer of approval in her dark eyes.

"Knows what?" He was going to pretend he didn't know what I meant. Probably because he wasn't one hundred percent sure and he didn't want to let slip anything until he knew for sure I had spilled the beans.

So I said explicitly, "I told Sophia I write the column."

Not even a hint of throbbing vein. He glanced at her with puppy dog eyes—*blecch.* "Cool. She won't tell anyone. I know the secret's safe with her."

Sophia smiled at him. "Yes. Would you like me to pinky swear with you, too, Tyler?"

For a minute I thought he'd suggest they use tongues instead, since his was hanging out. But no, he wasn't that far gone. Although, he held on to her pinky with his just a big longer than was necessary.

I'd been hoping for a scene. To be fired on the spot. But all I got was another one of those smiles (damn him and his Sophia-pinky-swearing-induced smile!) "So, when can I expect the column?"

Perversely, after protesting to Sophia that I didn't want to go back on my word, I worked up my courage to quit. To tell him I'd had enough. I didn't want to write the column—I didn't want to be Mother Hubbard anymore. It helped that he was trying hard not to steal too many glances at Sophia, who was watching us both with great amusement. "Tyler, I just don't think this is a good idea."

He shook his head, and I suddenly wished I had a rolled-up newspaper in my hand. "Of course it is."

"I—" I started to protest.

But then he turned his attention completely on me. His eyes were golden with sincerity. Or at least, that's my interpretation. "Katelyn, I've just been looking at this all wrong. Do you know, ever since you started the column, the papers have disappeared faster and we've had more hits on the Web site, as well? Mother Hubbard is huge."

"Are you insane? People are burning the paper on the library steps and nailing my column to the door with red paint on it!"

He ignored my well-thought-out objection. "I don't know why I didn't see it before. You just need to keep it going."

"By dating a loser and writing a column about it? I'm an advice columnist—think Dear Abby, not Singles Seen."

"I thought you might have trouble with the approach, that's why I dropped by." He said this while glancing nonchalantly (not) at Sophia. I think he liked that

Sophia knew. How sweet—he shared a secret with his crush.

Blecch. Tyler had seen the way Sophia goes through guys like a movie critic slices through the cheesy summer movies. But he still wanted her to look at him. Notice him. No doubt much more than that. Eww. I don't like where that thought takes me.

Not that I didn't understand the helpless compulsion he was under, though.

I shrugged, trying one more time to wiggle out of making the worst mistake of my life. "I just don't know what you want from me . . . or from Mother Hubbard, I should say."

"Never fear. Super Editor is here to rescue you, my dear." Tyler flipped open the laptop he'd carried under his arm, turned to Sophia, and handed her a twenty. "Can you get us some coffee? We're going to need it."

I had a flash of hope that Sophia would put him in his place and then cram the twenty into her bra. But she just nodded and headed off. It was anybody's guess whether she'd come back with coffee or not.

I had to feel sorry for Sophia—though, being the man magnet she was, not too sorry. I mean, I hate it when someone likes me more than I like them. Not that it has happened often. Twice that I know of, back in high school. One was a girl in my math class—definitely going nowhere, and she took it well, even though she did sit next to me in math class all senior year.

The other awkward moment was a boy, which is more on target, at least. He was sweet, good natured, funny . . . but there was no spark. I felt for him, really I did. At least once a month all four years of high school, he came close to asking me out, and then lost his nerve. It was an interesting and awkward little high school dance, watching him get his courage up to ask, and then change his mind.

I confess I helped discourage him as much as possible. I could always tell when he'd worked up enough nerve—his left eyebrow twitched. At the moment when he was about to ask, I'd come up with an insta-excuse about being unavailable. It got to be automatic with us—I didn't want to hurt him. Or alienate him either. I liked having him as a lab partner. He was smart with test tubes and Bunsen burners. No, I wasn't using him. I took great notes that usually got us extra points.

I have to say, there were times I was weak and tempted. He was such a nice guy. But when I say there was no spark, I mean none, zippo, nada. If we'd been the last couple standing on *Survivor*, we'd never have gotten a fire started. But we'd have shared our raw fish and coconuts well enough.

Richie was his name. And thinking of my ear as sexy was his fame. And I confess, when I heard he was going to my university, I was a bit worried that I'd still have to come up with the monthly excuse to keep him from asking me out.

But no. I'd seen him rarely. We didn't share any classes together, and our eating schedule was such that I saw him—to wave to across the crowded dining hall—only once or twice so far in a month. I guess it was because he was a theater major.

I'd seen his name listed in the paper for the fall production of *A Midsummer Night's Dream*. I'd been glad for him. He'd always had a flair for acting in our school productions, and he'd given me tickets to every performance. I'd gone, with my best friend, Claire. I thought that was sending a clear message—friends, no more than friends.

I was big on sending clear signals. It was a key part of my common-sense approach to dating. Now I just had to convince the campus I was right.

Tyler insisted I get started by laying the special editor's computer in my lap. Which meant he was really serious about this new column idea. "If you do a good job, we could have people not only burning our papers, but reading them too, by next week."

Maybe I would have refused. Maybe. But he smiled, and I started to type.

Dear Mother Hubbard,
WTF? Are you nuts? Why do you always insist that people throw out their date with the bad Chinese food?
The Entire Campus

Dear Entire Campus,
Okay. It has come to my attention

that a lot of you aren't fond of the common-sense approach to dating. Get over it. . . .

Just kidding.

Here's the way it is: Sometimes the writing is on the wall. Sometimes he just isn't going to call. Sometimes she hasn't really developed a migraine in the middle of dinner.

So why do you people keep holding on to a dead dream? Or if that's too negative for you, let me give it a positive spin. How come you don't drop the dead wood and reach out for another chance at some live stud or studette who won't make you feel like you've done something wrong?

Here's my philosophy in a nutshell: First Date: Meet, get to know each other. Goes well, keep going. Problems? For anything less than a total eclipse of the sun, give the guy a second chance. After all, doesn't everybody deserve a second chance?

The second date, though. That's where you separate the boys from the men (or the jerks from the good guys). If he dribbles, if he drools, if he calls you babe, the third-date rule kicks in—run for your life!

Now, MH knows that hormones sometimes muddy the common sense we were all born with. That's what the third-date rule is meant to counter. After all, if he doesn't pass muster on the second date, no matter how hard your heart is beating, you just don't go there. Eventually your heart slows down and you find the next one to take for a two-date test run.

Simple, *non?* So why don't you believe it? Because you don't have any experience listening to your head instead of your hormones.

Our esteemed managing editor has persuaded me to give you that experience—vicariously. I'm going to pick one of my two-date losers and try out a third date. Happy now? Good.

Stay tuned for details next week.
Mother Hubbard

• • •

"Satisfied?" I handed the laptop back over to Tyler.

He read the column quickly. "It's a little long, but I think I can make the space for it, since it's important."

"Yeah. Important. The students on campus won't sleep until they read my column." I couldn't help sounding a little snarky. We'd just spent some dedicated time huddled over Tyler's laptop, without Sophia or the coffee Tyler had asked her to get. And he was still grinning at me like I was his best bud. His little sister. It was me and David Morse all over again.

"Wouldn't that be great?" He grinned and nodded as he safely closed the file and turned off his laptop. "People looking forward to the next issue?"

"And if it doesn't work? Will I have to videotape my next date, after carefully disguising myself with a paper bag over my head?"

"I know this will do it. I can feel it— and you know what they say about editorial instinct."

"No, I don't know. But I could guess— it isn't infallible?" Any more snarky and he could have cut himself on my commentary. Not that he noticed. Did that mean he really liked me, so he could ignore it, like he ignored the fact that Sophia had absconded with his twenty bucks? Or did it just mean he didn't care?

Who can tell? He just grinned again, like he knew something I didn't. "Everyone will be looking forward to next week's column when you have to eat your words."

"Says you." I had no intention of eating my words. I was right and I wasn't going to be meek about sharing that information after what would no doubt be an absolutely disastrous date. After all, I knew who the lucky date-winner was going to be. I'd chosen a guy who couldn't deliver a good date if he had an instruction manual handy. Not that I was going to share that secret with anyone, pinky swear or not.

Six

"You're not going on your date in that?" Sophia looked as disapproving as my mother usually did when she saw me getting ready to go out.

"What?" I looked down at my jeans—they were clean. My top was a new cute black lace one my mom had bought when she visited for parents' weekend. I'd even exchanged my more comfortable sneakers for a pair of strappy sandals with two-inch heels. "I've got earrings on, for heaven's sake. What's wrong with the way I look?"

"There's nothing wrong with the way you look—if you're going to class. But for a date? Do you want the guy to think you've already written him off before the evening even begins?"

Well, yes, I did. But, again, that wasn't something I was about to confess. "I'm going for a statement of casual fun, not full-on commitment. Guys don't even like that, anyway."

She wrinkled her nose at me. Apparently my answer was unsatisfactory for a woman of any age or reluctance. "They want you to care."

The last thing I wanted to do was argue about what I looked like going on the date I didn't want to go on in the first place with a guy I was sure was a dead end—except that he'd serve a purpose for the column I would write for Tyler. "What would you suggest?"

She looked me over carefully. "The top is okay, but you need a better bra."

Great. Was I supposed to go shopping for this dead-end date too? "I don't have a better bra. And I don't have time to get one. I'm supposed to meet him out in front of the dorm in half an hour."

She frowned, thinking. "Borrow one of mine."

"Is that a joke? You're at least a 34C and I'm a 34B if I'm lucky."

She began to rummage through her drawers and I feared she was going to pull out a bra and a pair of socks for me to stuff it with. But when she turned around she was only holding a lacy black bra with solid lift factor. "Here, you can have this one. I ordered it online and they sent me the wrong size. I'll never get around to returning it."

It was a gorgeous bra. Made me actually look like I had more than just best-friend breasts, but didn't pinch or smush anything sideways. I was perky, even. "Okay. Thanks. I concede this was a good change."

She smiled and nodded in approval. But then the frown came back.

What? The bra had made a major difference. Hadn't I given her that point? I'd have to be blind not to, since I could see in the mirror that I looked just a touch sexier. Who knew a good bra could do that? I mean, it's covered up by a shirt!

But Sophia had moved on from the bra. "Are you wearing makeup?"

"Can't you tell?"

She examined me critically close up. "Mascara. Gloss. Not enough." She whipped out her makeup case and spread it open on her bed. "Sit."

I perched obediently on the edge of her bed while Sophia patted and brushed and smoothed and, in the end, made me look like a zillion bucks with her fancy Italian makeup.

She let me keep the top, but made me exchange the jeans for a skirt my mom had bought me that I'd sworn I'd never wear because it exposed my fat thighs. Sophia told me I was cute in it. And when I looked in the mirror, I actually agreed.

I also agreed that I looked like a girl who wanted to hang out with someone special, not just any guy I happened to stumble over. Even though I hadn't really changed my inner attitude, it was no longer reflected in the outer me. I suppose that was a good thing, since there wasn't a minute to spare and I scurried out to the front steps of the dorm to await the unsuspecting guy who was going to be featured in my column next week. Anonymously, of course.

He drove up right on time. A miracle. He waved and popped the passenger door of his very old, very noisy—not to mention vibrating—car. He didn't get out, but he smiled at me and said, "Hey, you look great. Come on, get in."

My first inclination was to run back into the dorm, screaming. He couldn't follow me, since the doors were always kept locked for security—when someone hadn't propped them open with a textbook, of course. But then I'd have to explain my freak-out not only to Tyler, but to Sophia, too.

So I got in and used the open window to get a grip and close the door, since it seemed to have lost its handle a long time ago. I thought, briefly, about all those horror movies where the girls get locked in a car with a psycho.

But Todd wasn't a psycho. He just didn't have a lot of money to spend on a car right now since he was working in the dining hall making minimum wage. I knew from his Web page, and our last two dates, that he spent most of his money on music and Starbucks, the fuel that got him through the engineering classes he hated.

Don't get me wrong, I'm not saying Todd was a bad guy. For someone else. One day he'd make a great husband for a woman who was organized, driven, and tolerant. But as a boyfriend he was lacking most of my basic requirements. He didn't listen well, he didn't explain himself at all, and if he considered other people's feelings, it was by accident.

Given our history, I was not expecting to enjoy this date. More like I was hoping I'd survive it without going nuclear.

The first time we hung out, it had been with a bunch of friends at the small bowling alley on campus. Tenpin bowling, which he had never done before. He'd always bowled candlestick, which I'd never heard of before (nor did I hear of it from him—hence the reason I know he doesn't explain himself). "This isn't bowling. It's stupid." Repeated over and over again during the night. I explained—we all explained—the game to him, yet he still got confused.

But that was just the first date. He hadn't spit on me or had a public meltdown, so he deserved a second chance. But not bowling. Definitely not bowling.

He hadn't argued when I suggested we try a movie the next time we hung out. I was thinking that he had to know what a movie was. In fact, I knew he did.

Confession time: The Web is a wonderful tool for the dating girl. Turns out Todd had a blog. And a Web site (big plus) that showcased his interest in model trains (not a plus). In my defense, I'm not the only girl on campus who does this. Technology is meant to make our lives easier, after all. So for me, cute guy equals a little Google session.

Besides, picking a movie can be tricky when you don't know each other well. My snoop session made it easy. Todd was interested in trains. It so happened there was a movie playing about a runaway train. It was action, romance, and trains. What could go wrong? Let me count the ways.

He picked me up late. Not his fault. Unless you count against him buying a car that only liked to start every other day. I didn't. But I considered it when he pulled up in a wreck that was belching black smoke.

And it went downhill from there. Believe me. Not only did he leave me to figure out his ancient malfunctioning car door handle for myself, he ate almost all of the popcorn before I could get my hand in edgewise.

So anyone would understand why I wasn't pumped for a third date. Once again I'd chosen a movie. Not a train theme, but a chick flick—hey, I wasn't expecting to enjoy the guy, so why not enjoy the film?

What made it all 10 zillion times worse was that I had to do the asking because I was on a timetable and Todd didn't have a clue that he was being used to prove a point. I had suggested to Tyler that I simply hang around the area of the dining hall where he liked to eat lunch. I figured if I smiled and talked to him there was a good chance he'd ask me out again. Eventually. Some girls are brave. Me, I'm a coward. I prefer to back my way into a relationship under cover of a friendship if I have to do the maneuvering.

But both Sophia and Tyler had pointed out that this was not likely to get me a date for the weekend—which would leave me (and the readers waiting for Mother Hubbard to prove herself wrong) without a column next week.

One thing I know. I'm more like Mother Hubbard than even I realized. I really hated asking him out. That stomach squeezing moment when he was filling up his milk glass and I wasn't sure if he'd say yes was awful. Not to mention hard on the pocketbook when he stood back and let me pay for the tickets. And the popcorn. And the soda.

I guess I can see why guys might like to abandon the old-fashioned notion of asking a girl on a date and paying for everything. Not to mention being chewed over by her father and cooed over by her camera-snapping mom. At least in college, there's no chance of that happening, no matter how old-fashioned the date happens to be.

The theme of Todd's and my third date seemed to be me in charge and him following like a sheep. I picked out seats on the aisle because there was a bit of aisle light to discourage him from deciding I'd invited him to a make-out session. That was definitely not happening. He did at least carry his own popcorn and soda.

There were only four other people in the theater—two couples much like me and my date.

Except for the fact that they looked like they were still in high school. It seemed fitting, given the immaturity of my own date. On the other hand, it was also awkward; the other two couples weren't exactly interested in the movie, as evidenced by the kissing and giggling sounds coming from the opposite dark corners they had settled themselves into.

The movie was good. I laughed. Todd didn't. But he didn't snore, either. I think he had started to put his arm around my shoulder once. Probably when the noise from the dark corners of the theater inspired him. Fortunately, I was able to head him off by leaning forward and tying my shoe until the urge passed and he sat back to stuff a big handful of popcorn in his mouth.

As soon as the credits started rolling, I started worrying. Would it be horrible to tell him to just take me home? I didn't want to get stuck paying for him to eat a burger. I'd paid enough for the movie and I had plenty of material for my column—enough to convince all the readers that I was right not to date this guy again.

As we got up to leave, I attempted to break what was becoming an awkward silence. "So, did you like it?"

"No."

What to answer to that? He couldn't even muster the effort to tell a polite lie? "I did. I'm really glad I picked this one." Take that, bad date guy. I didn't even apologize for his hating it. Why should I tell a polite lie if he wasn't going to bother?

He didn't reply. He had more important things on his mind, apparently. "Want to get something to eat?" He looked a little hopeful, and I didn't doubt, from the way he'd plowed through his popcorn, that he was still hungry. Guys were bottomless pits. Maybe that's why in the olden days they were the ones who paid for the food.

A few excuses ran through my mind. But I didn't use them. I just echoed him instead. "No."

"Okay." He didn't say anything else as we drove home. Not that he seemed mad or anything either. He turned on music and hummed to it a little. Every so often he took his hands off the wheel to play the air guitar at some riff that called to him.

There was the awkward end-of-date moment when the question about whether he'd try to kiss me hung in the air. I had a little trouble getting the car door open. I wanted to escape any possibility of a kiss so badly that my fingers were sweaty and I couldn't find the latch buried in the hole in the door.

He had his seat belt off and had slid over the bench seat to sit beside me. I was afraid I wasn't going to avoid the kiss, but all he did was reach over and open the door. "It's a little tricky."

Tell me about it. I leaped out of the car and then turned around, feeling unaccountably guilty. "Thanks for everything."

He smiled as if he hadn't been on the same date as I had. "Thanks for asking me out. I've never been asked out before. It was cool."

There was nothing to say to that but

"Great, see you around." Like I said, he was a nice enough guy, but he needed a tougher woman than I was to whip him into boyfriend material.

Sophia was out when I got up to the room. Good. I took one look in the mirror—I still, after all that, looked like a girl who wanted to go out. Interesting what makeup can do when wielded by skilled hands. I was going to have to get Sophia to show me how to do it myself.

I headed down to the commons room. Without Sophia I couldn't unload about my date much, though. All that hush-hush stuff about Mother Hubbard. But I could share some details and get some sympathy from the girls who hadn't had anything too fun to keep them out late tonight.

There were three girls in sweats and no makeup lounging in the commons. They were watching a makeover show and drinking from a big pitcher of something fruity. After half a semester in the dorm, I knew to come prepared. I filled up my trusty coffee mug and plopped down on a sturdy yet totally uncomfortable orange chair. Clearly the university did not want to tempt us to tote off the furniture if any of us decided to leave dorm living for an apartment of our own.

"Home already? Sophia said you had a hottie on the hook."

I took a swig from my mug. "Not hot. So I unhooked him and threw him back."

"Had to be bad if you'd rather be here, watching strangers get a makeover with us."

"It was."

The third date had been awkward, painful, and useless. I had been right. Everyone would have to believe Mother Hubbard's wisdom now.

Seven

Tyler had no intention of letting me write the third-date project off before he could assess it himself.

He had arranged to meet me at the campus Starbucks for a copy of the column outlining my worst third date ever.

He took the flash drive and plugged the file into his laptop, but without even looking at my column, he demanded, "Details."

Right. Like I wanted to talk to Tyler about my date. "It's a column, Tyler, not a novel. Besides, this is a small campus. The more detail, the more likely the guy in question will be easily identified. I don't want him, but I don't want to kill his dating chances forever."

He grinned. "That's what 'names have been changed to protect the innocent' is for. Change the details." He scanned to see if our isolated corner table was isolated enough. Except for a couple of football players who were occupied in an arm wrestling match on the other side of the room and didn't even seem to notice us, we were effectively alone.

Satisfied that we were not in any way being spied upon, Tyler leaned forward. "The details are for me."

"Why?" I didn't like the thought of giving him a chance to see me in dating mode without even asking me out. It seemed . . . perverted.

"We're friends, aren't we?"

I didn't scream. I hate those words, but I didn't scream. It was so undignified. "What does our being friends have to do with it?" Besides meaning that he didn't see me as possible girlfriend/hot date material? Not that I would admit that aloud.

"The whole point of this dating thing is that you give guys a real chance. How will

I know if you have if you don't give me the details?" Right. I didn't know if he was onto me, or if he really did have great editorial talent. And I didn't care at this moment, as long as I could convince him I'd proved Mother Hubbard was right.

I leaned in, like I was going to whisper a secret to him. "You said we're friends, right?"

"Of course we are." He nodded warily.

"Good!" I sat back with a big smile and my arms crossed to indicate that Fort Katelyn was locked and bolted shut on all extraneous dating details. "Well, friends trust each other."

He looked at my crossed arms for a moment, but then just smiled and shook his head. "Are you from planet clueless, princess? Friends don't trust each other, they test each other."

"I'm not that cynical." Well, yes I am sometimes. But I wasn't going to admit it to Tyler.

"Well, I am. So spill." Without waiting for me to confirm I wasn't saying anything, he took my backpack and started rummaging through it without permission.

"Hey. Get out of there." I grabbed it and tugged it back. I didn't care if we were friends, there are just things in a girl's backpack she doesn't want any guy to see.

He gave up the backpack easily and I almost fell on the floor with it. We'd caught the attention of the arm wrestlers for a moment. But when they saw we weren't going to get into a fight, they stopped watching us.

I saw why Tyler hadn't fought harder. He had what he wanted. My little pink book.

He thumbed through. "Where is this guy, anyway? I can't read your code."

"You're not supposed to be able to understand it. That would defeat the purpose." Not to mention that Tyler's being able to read my code would be more in the realm of dangerous and uncomfortable in light of one particular entry.

I snatched the book back. "Here." I flipped to the page. "He's this one." I tapped my finger on Todd's entry. He doesn't think about his date, complains a lot, and . . ." I grabbed a pen and added a code. ". . . and he lets the girl pay without even offering to pay for himself." Then I put the book back into my backpack and held it tightly in my lap. I wasn't going to let another smash and grab attempt happen if I could help it.

"You picked 'Looking For a Mom' as your third date?"

"Yes. I did. And it didn't work out." I didn't like his tone, but I pretended not to understand why he was looking at me like I'd gotten caught cheating on an exam.

"No kidding."

"Look, he was a loser, okay? We went to a movie and he had to go to the bathroom three times. I smelled Milk Duds on his breath the second time he came back. And then afterward, when we were driving home, I tried to talk to him about the movie, and all he could say was 'My seat kept squeaking.'"

Tyler eyed my backpack, and then the arm wrestlers over in the corner. "I take it he's not getting a fourth date?"

"Not a chance. I knew that before, though, but I hope I've proved it to them." I gestured widely to indicate the entire campus.

"We'll see." Tyler looked at me. I didn't

like the suspicion in his eyes. "Did you sabotage the date, Katelyn?"

"Of course I didn't!"

He looked skeptical.

"Ask Sophia. When I walked out of that dorm I was dressed like a girl who wanted to go out and have fun." Which was nothing but the simple truth.

He shrugged and tapped his laptop. "I'm not the one you have to convince." He eyed my backpack again, and I wondered if I should start leaving my little pink book at home from now on.

"The public will back me. Wait until you read the column to criticize it, please, Mr. Editor Man." I tried a little Sookie-style intimidation.

I don't think it worked, because he just blinked my comment away and asked, "Who's number two?"

My first answer, completely off topic, was that I was number two. Forever destined to be on the sidelines of love. But then I realized what he meant. He wanted to know who was next on my list for the third date circus he had me putting on. "I haven't decided."

"You have to. This column will work for this week, but we need another one for next week. Which means a date this weekend at the latest."

"What if the campus response is in my favor? Why keep going?"

"We told the readers—"

"No. I only said I was going to go on one third date."

He looked at me as if he didn't know whether to compliment my clever attempt to circumvent two-thirds of his idea or choke me. Naturally, I voted for compliment. In fact, falling in love with me over the column would be nice, too. As if.

He shook his head. "I told Professor Golding and everybody in Human Sexuality. They're expecting three third dates— it's more statistically sound, remember?"

"Right." Honestly, I was hoping I'd prove my point with this column. That the students would speak out and absolve me (or Mother Hubbard, at least) of any advisory wrongdoing. But there was no point in telling him that. He enjoyed the controversy. It wasn't his dating life on trial, after all.

●●●

Names have been changed to protect the innocent. I will refer to the first candidate as Third Date #1. Third Date #1 and I went to a movie about cars. The big box of Raisinets was shared . . . 90-10. Me being on the 10 percent end.

I had begun my column with that disclaimer to head off Todd's recognizing himself, or anyone else's recognizing him from what I said, but do you think anyone paid attention? Of course not.

The replies that followed my faithful, if artfully disguised, rendition of my date were annoying. Not that I needed to see them. Or wanted to see them. But Tyler forwarded the e-mails to me as soon as he read them. With gleeful little comments like, "This one really loves you." The notes he saved to deliver in a pizza box so people in the dorm would be none the wiser.

After a while the comments blurred together, forming an impression in my mind that went something like this:

Whatz damatta you? Don't you believe in love? Maybe he had some bad Mexican food and didn't want to gross you out. You women want everything—bet he paid for the tickets and the popcorn, too, and that's one of the facts you changed to protect the truth, huh?

Since the paper had reimbursed me for the date with Looking For a Man (which I hadn't known until Tyler asked me how much I'd spent), I wanted to set the record straight about the money. But Tyler didn't want to start any controversy about how he expended his budget.

Of course, those were the guys. Who, it seemed, tended to think of themselves as Third Date #1. I had a feeling there were many women on campus who weren't going to get calls for another date. But what could I do about that?

The women fell into another sphere altogether:

(from the softer side of girls)
How could you not let him choose

the film? And why would you sneak out to get your own popcorn and scarf it down in the bathroom? It's much nicer to share—you don't look like such a pig.

(from the more firm perspective) Good for you that you picked a movie you liked. But why didn't you demand equal candy time instead of sneaking out to the counter? How's he going to learn how to share?

"What do they want from me?" I had called Tyler for an emergency meeting in the library near the engineering periodicals. Not a popular spot unless you were an engineer—and I, even as a freshman, knew it wasn't likely any of them read the school newspaper or knew who Mother Hubbard was.

"The guys want you to cut them some slack and the girls want you to be a warrior princess when it comes to taking back the date."

"Don't forget the girls who want me to be Campus Barbie."

"Or the guys who want to date you." He grinned.

"What guys?"

He blinked sheepishly. "Oh, I must have left those out."

"Oh, well. Easy, then. I'll just clone myself and have at pleasing all the people all the time." I rolled my eyes at him. "Look, I don't think this is going well. Everyone seems more angry rather than less so. Probably we should just give up the experiment."

I had expected him to be annoyed, but he wasn't. He was curt. Like I'd done something wrong. "Give up? Like you do with the guys you date?"

"Hey, what room do you have to talk? I haven't seen you with any girls on a steady basis." Unless you counted Sophia. Who thought of him as an adorable friendly teddy bear who sometimes brought over late-night pizza when she was hungry.

"Look at this." He slid a printed e-mail across the table to me. It had been sent anonymously, so it was someone who either knew computers or knew someone who did. Great. Only 90 percent of the campus fell into that category.

> Hey, Mother Hubbard. Just how many guys did you get to third date with in high school, anyway? Sounds to me like you wouldn't give the pope a third chance.

"The pope doesn't date." It was all I could think of to say. I certainly wasn't going to tell anyone that I'd never had a third date until forced to by a vocal minority of the campus who actually read the rag Tyler published.

I barely liked to admit that shameful fact to myself. I preferred the head-in-sand method of dealing with my poor dating record and habit of crushing hard on someone who wouldn't ask me out if I were the last woman on earth.

"You are pretty harsh for someone who's never had a steady boyfriend."

I think I preferred Tyler better when he was less insightful. "You don't know I've never had a steady boyfriend."

"I met you the first day of school,

remember? When the upperclassmen helped the freshmen move in and you dropped that box of books on my foot."

Yes. I did remember that day, as it happens. I had dropped the box on his foot because he had been so busy staring at Sophia's tight white T-shirt that he had almost closed the door on me.

I blinked at him as if I were trying to dredge up my memories from all the way back at the beginning of the semester. "No? I forgot. Did I?"

"Yes. You did. And I've never seen you making goo-goo eyes at anyone in almost two months. In fact, my keen journalistic spidey sense bets you never have—not even in high school."

"Goo-goo eyes?" I made the opposite of goo-goo eyes at him. Or at least, I tried. "I don't believe I need to make goo goo eyes to hook up."

"Seriously, Katelyn. You're supposed to write an advice column for people with life and relationship problems." Whoa. Tyler was really concerned about this. He had his managing editor face on. "But if you don't have any practical experience—"

Could life get any more unfair? "You're the one who begged me to write the column, remember?" I protested, thinking the only thing needed to make this moment perfect was for me to blurt out that I'd only accepted because I wanted to be near him. I bit my tongue, hard, to make sure that didn't happen.

He held up his hands, backing off a little. "I know. I know. But I couldn't get anyone else to do it. And you're reliable. If you could just loosen up a little, everything would be great."

"I have no intention of loosening up my common sense. If you don't want me to continue with the column, fine. Then just tell me so and I'll be happy to stop writing this stupid thing and hearing all the half-baked gripings of a group who wouldn't know love if it bit them on the butt."

"Okay." For a minute I thought we were done. Really done. But then he put on his concerned editor's face again. "If you've ever been in a real relationship."

"What are you talking about?" I tried to bluff, but my voice shook a little. I hadn't expected the question.

"Have you?"

"Have I what?" Lame, I know. But I do have that hopeful streak, and it was praying I could put off answering until a meteor struck the earth and obliterated us all.

He stood his ground, though. "Have you *ever* been on a third date before Looking For a Mom?"

Eight

Once, long ago, my sixth-grade gym teacher, who had a gorilla-size chip on her shoulder, gave us girls two pieces of advice: The best defense is a good offense, and never let a guy tower over you in an argument—it gives him the psychological advantage. She was fired shortly after that, for tipping our principal, Mr. Mandis, into a Dumpster, so the advice really stuck in my mind.

I stood up, put my backpack on the table, and faced Tyler down. Maybe not such a good idea, since my knees, I discovered, were shaking. Where was a good shot of adrenaline when I needed it?

He laughed. "It's not a hard question, Katelyn." Apparently, Tyler found my refusal to answer funny. "Yes. No. No big deal if you're the pickiest dater on the planet. It would explain a lot of this wacko Mother Hubbard advice you've been giving, to tell the truth."

Turns out, anger is a good source of adrenaline. "You didn't know me in high school. You haven't known me very long. So what if I haven't rushed into a relationship? I have classes to study for and a career to plan. How dare you assume I've never been on a third date?" Another plus to anger is that the truth is easy to hide behind outrage. Like, I wasted four years in high school hanging out with a guy who wasn't ever going to like me like I liked him. There had been some guys who might have liked me. But I hadn't really given them a chance. Which didn't really mean my three-date rule was dumb. Just that I hadn't practiced it on enough guys. Yet.

He stepped back, as if he thought I might morph into vampire girl and bite his throat out. "True. I haven't known you very long. Maybe you were homecoming queen and planning to marry the homecoming king until he dumped you for your English teacher."

He'd come a little too close to the truth. But I could see it was by accident. He had no clue who David Morse was—let alone that he was indeed homecoming king. The smile on his face had slid sideways and he looked a little sick. I realized he was sorry he'd insulted me, and my own anger started to slip away.

Too soon, it turned out, because he continued, "But I think I should be the one to pick the next two guys you go out on a third date with."

"I've already got one picked out." The perfect one to make my case to the campus. Slacker Dude. No way was Tyler taking him away from me. No one would expect me to go on a fourth date with a guy who had an imaginary friend who'd come to college with him to "make sure I study hard and make my parents proud."

"Is he someone Sophia would date?"

"Who cares?"

"The readers care. So, is he someone Sophia would date?"

Never in a million years. "How would I know?" I asked that with a straight face because I was certain Tyler had no idea that when Slacker Dude had come to the room to pick me up for our coffee date, Sophia had actually faked a phone call on her cell and tried to convince my date that my mother was in the hospital awaiting surgery.

I'd told him she was a little bit crazy, which he understood—all too well, as I discovered throughout the evening. He hadn't even had a second date. But I didn't have to tell that to Tyler.

He shrugged. "Okay. I'll just ask her."

"That's not fair."

"Why? Because you picked a guy who was Most Likely to Fail as Third Date #1 and you don't want anyone to interfere with your agenda?"

"I . . . didn't." Even I didn't believe me.

"Still." He reached for my backpack, which I had foolishly left unprotected on the top of the table. "I think I'll pick from now on."

I watched in horror as he once again took out my little pink book and began to thumb through. But all I could think of was that I couldn't let him randomly choose the next guy for me to have a third date with.

He opened the book and frowned. "Are there pages missing?"

"No," I lied, looking straight into his eyes with a sincere frown of puzzlement that he would even ask.

"Good. Then explain this code of yours to me."

I took a deep breath, as if to protest, and then I gave up. What can I say? I'm a good friend, even to high school homecoming kings who have the hots for their history (not English) teacher. How can I possibly be expected to change only halfway through my first semester in college?

"It's pretty simple. I pick a code name, just in case anyone—like you—ever gets their hands on my book. And then I rate them on ten simple points."

"Ten points?" He checked over the book and slowly said, "*S, D, E, T, L, C, M, H, IQ, B.*" He looked up, a puzzled frown on his face. "What do those mean?"

I said quickly, "Sense of humor. Where we go. Who pays. Whether he talks. Whether he listens. If he wears clean clothes. If he has an interesting major. What his favorite hobby is. If he's smart. The usual."

Tyler had been paying attention, even though I'd rattled off my list rather quickly. "That's only nine. What's the tenth point—" he checked the book. "*B*. What's *B* stand for?"

Buzz factor. Like when a cute guy is around and you feel the temperature rise and the buzz in your ears gets so loud that it shuts out everything but your hot guy radar. But I wasn't going to admit that to him. "Whether he has an interesting blog," I lied rather lamely.

Fortunately, Tyler didn't notice the lapse in logic. "Okay." He started to read with a furrowed brow. It's hard to tell much from this," he finally said. I mean, you like Mellow Man's hobby, because you gave it a nine, but it could be grave robbing for all I can tell."

I glanced at the entry. "He paints. I like a guy with an artistic flair."

"Do you?" For a moment he was looking at me. Me me, not Katelyn the best friend and chump, but Katelyn the girl who liked things he didn't know about. "What other hobbies do you rate highly?"

I froze. There's this thing about guys who generate a buzz factor off the scale. For example, Tyler. You want them to notice you. But then, when they do, you worry that you'll blow it by saying something stupid. I tried an evasive maneuver. I shrugged. "I like lots of things."

"What's your top favorite hobby for a guy?"

Reluctantly, I told him the truth. "Working on his car."

"Really? Why?" He seemed surprised. Maybe a little disappointed? I remembered too late that he didn't even have a car. He went everywhere on his bicycle. Which was why he had such a nice firm butt. Not that I'd noticed or anything.

I tried to fix my mistake. "Guys who love their cars, and take care of them well. You can tell they'll treat a girl right. But the same holds true for guys who love their bikes." Yeah. Lame. I know. But that's hope springing eternal for you.

"That's Katelyn logic for you." I couldn't tell if he meant it in a good way or a bad way, because his smile was a little forced. "What's your least favorite?"

Oh, great. Another minefield and I wasn't even sure yet I hadn't just gotten blown up in the last one. "Bodybuilding."

"You don't like guys who go to the gym?"

Tyler went to the gym every morning. That's his serious side coming out—when he believes in something, he puts it on a to-do list and does it. Who couldn't love a guy like that?

I plunged on, despite the warning in my brain that I should quit now. "Of course I believe in going to the gym and being healthy. I'm talking about those guys who spend four hours there and then have to talk about the size of their biceps all the time." I crossed my fingers. I'd never heard Tyler once ask anyone to feel his bicep.

Bingo. He nodded. "Oh. Them. I hate them too. What a waste of testosterone."

Yay! Score one for Katelyn. "Exactly."

"Okay. I won't pick a guy who has any hobbies that might include bodybuilding." He glanced up. "Do you care about the IQ rating? It is college, after all. Aren't we all smart?"

I shrugged. "Some smart people can be awfully dumb. The smartest guy in school could decide to take me on a date to toilet paper a professor's house."

"No way."

"Way. At least, it happened to a friend of mine in high school."

He bent back to the book, mumbling to himself, "S, D, E, T, L, C, M, H, IQ, B . . ."

I thought I was glad he had believed me about the last little rating point. Until his finger stopped on a guy who had a really good buzz factor rating. "You liked this Hands-On Guy's blog a lot; you gave him a ten. And he has a five in the IQ category, which means he doesn't expect to go toilet papering with a cute girl. Let's give him a third chance."

Tyler was smiling at me. And he was still talking. But the buzzing in my ears was very loud and I was busy trying to digest that he'd just picked Hands-On Guy—otherwise known as Blaine—out for my next third date.

Blaine.

With buzz factor out the wazoo. I mean, the guy had the hottie quotient of a movie star. Which meant he was constantly hooking up—and well schooled in the art. I tried to think of a worse choice for a third date I'd not only have to survive, but have to write about for the entire student population.

I couldn't think of one.

Not even Tyler himself.

Oh, goody.

Don't get me wrong, it wasn't that I was so into Blaine. I wasn't. He was out of my league, and even my inner buzzometer knew that the first time I saw him.

What can I say about him that his name doesn't already reflect? Born in pretension, raised in pretension, life was good for this guy. And he wanted to share that goodness with every female on campus.

The problem with Blaine was that he was not just a 24 carat jerk, he was also a very sexy 24 carat jerk.

Why do human beings lose their common sense when a cute date prospect shows the slightest interest? Or even more critical to me, why do I have to fight my better instincts when a guy with top buzz factor and absolutely no scruples wants to put his hand on my knee?

Someone had asked Professor Golding this question. I don't know if she saw all the girls lean forward a little breathlessly for the secret, but she only used the moment for a joke. "Because otherwise our species is doomed." At least, I hope it was a joke. She got a laugh from the class, although it was a little bit nervous and not that loud.

And don't think that just because the perennial best-friend girl doesn't throw her bra and phone number at the hot guy, that doesn't mean she's not just as affected as those girls who do. No way. Nuh-uh. We just hide it better. I suppose guys have the same problem, but I'm much more intimately aware of the female side of the attraction equation.

Blaine had a radar for girls who had interest. And, oddly enough for his type, he didn't stick only with the beautiful people. He was willing to take a chance on girls who hadn't been cheerleaders or homecoming queens. Girls like me, in other words.

I'd noticed him in calculus on that first day when we were all still recovering from the shock of an expensive dictionary-size book full of numbers, letters, and Greek symbols like pi and beta.

Blaine sat a row ahead of me and just to the left, so that I found myself paying less attention to the professor and more attention to the appealing nature of Blaine's profile. I wanted to know what color his eyes were. I thought I'd caught a flash of green, an unusual color, and I was unable to concentrate on calculus until I had an answer to the most burning question in my mind that morning.

When someone behind us came in late, Blaine turned to look and caught my rather blatant stare.

My first thought was *Yep, green, just like I thought.* My second was *Uh-oh.*

But he smiled, and then he smiled a little more widely while I recovered from the blush that covered me from forehead to neckline. So I smiled back.

After class he asked me to have lunch with him. I accepted, even though technically it was a no-fault date, since we both had dining hall tickets and our parents had paid for them.

He did scoop the biggest brownie onto my plate and filled my glass with his special mixture of Mountain Dew, Diet Pepsi, and a smidge of Dr Pepper. He called it Blaine's Brew.

Something in the back of my mind warned me that such a cute guy coming on so strong was worth putting up the caution flags. But all my attempts to deflect his charm with my best-friend moves were ineffective.

He just wouldn't treat me like a sidekick and insisted on treating me like a date. Not even like the cheap date my dining hall meal plan made me.

I think, if things had gone just a little differently on the second date, I might actually have gone for the third date with Blaine. But luck was with me the second time he asked me out—to a frat party.

Blaine, a sophomore, belonged already and was past the ugly pledge stage. I didn't have to picture him rushing if I didn't want to, which was a relief because I find the whole fraternity/sorority rushing scene a little junior high.

Call me shallow, but I just didn't think I could date a guy if I knew he was going through hell week and all that entailed. It has something to do with the gross activities they make the pledges do. The admin types were always coming down on the fraternities for some sketchy behavior.

Like keggers. Which they certainly had, but more discreetly, as I discovered when Blaine brought me to the Sigma Alpha Gamma house.

"Sounds like our calculus textbook," I joked when I saw the five-foot-high sign in front of the driveway. I'd been feeling a little light-headed from all the attention. He'd picked me up at the dorm, and in the process charming Sophia into taking me aside and whispering, "This one, he is adorable, but be careful, sweetie."

He'd draped his arm over my shoulder and pulled me close as we walked, and I couldn't help but notice that we got some jealous stares from a few people hurrying along dateless to the library. So I thought my joking would be appropriate. Really, I did.

"What sounds like calculus?"

"Sigma Alpha Gamma."

He looked at the sign, looked at me smiling at him, feeling absolutely comfortable. Then he dropped his arm from my shoulder and stalked away without another word. I'd heard guys could be funny about their frats. But still.

The warm feeling had frozen over in the blink of an eye. I knew enough about guys to know I was supposed to run after him and beg for forgiveness. But I didn't want to. Okay, I did want to, but since he'd turned the charm off, my common sense exerted itself with a statement along the lines of *What a jerk to be upset about three stupid Greek letters—that* are *used in calculus.*

I didn't know what else to do, so I went into the frat house and took the beer that some guy with a hose shoved in my hand. It was loud and dark. I saw Blaine once and waved. It wasn't an apology wave, just an *I see you* wave. He was not amused and let me know it by ignoring me all evening . . . or at least for the half an hour I stayed before walking home alone.

So you can understand why I looked at Tyler, sitting there with my little pink book in his hand, and I crossed my arms and said, "No. Absolutely not."

Nine

Apparently, my Buddha statue refusal was like waving a red cape at a bull. Because he crossed his arms too. "It's Hands-On Guy, or I'll put a column in the paper about how Mother Hubbard hasn't ever been on a third date. Maybe I'll even tell them who she is."

Guys. They didn't even need a gym teacher to tell them the secret of a good defense was a good offense.

But I wasn't biting. He was bluffing. He had to be. Outing Mother Hubbard would cost him more than it would me. I hoped.

"No."

Annoyingly, he continued his bluff. "Hands-On Guy or you're a campus-wide unsecret."

I wasn't going to go out with Blaine. So I called his bluff. I gave him my column, with Mother Hubbard's explanation for why the experiment was over. No more third dates. It was a great column, and I kind of hoped it would make Tyler smile at me again.

Too bad for me, he called mine, too.

Tyler didn't run my column. He ran his own. He called it "Mother Hubbard Checks Out" and told everything about how I'd chickened out. He came just short of revealing the secret identity of Mother Hubbard, which he apparently had too much sense to do. No, he just told everyone that Mother Hubbard refused to go out with Hands-On Guy.

My favorite line of the whole infuriating column was this one:

It is this editor's opinion that Mother Hubbard hasn't been on a third date in her first one hundred years. And if the campus can't convince her to go out with Hands-On Guy, she'll spend the next hundred years only getting to second date.

Maybe I wouldn't have cared. Maybe I would have simply moved on with my life without Mother Hubbard and Tyler. Maybe. If he hadn't forwarded me the responses from other students on campus. I call them responses, but they were more like taunts—or threats.

Even the few relatively nice responses didn't take my side. The girls thought I needed to give Hands-On Guy a chance. One advised me if I ever wanted to find "the one," I needed to date guys who were so different from me they made my head spin. The "opposites attract until you puke" philosophy at work, I guess.

But the guys—the guys thought I was a man hater. Ironically, they then proceeded to give me lots of reasons to become a man hater. But still, a few guys made one compelling point that got me to throw myself on the mercy of the campus.

Especially since I wasn't about to get any mercy from Tyler.

So, Miss Big Shot
Why don't you want to go on third dates? What can it hurt? Guys have feelings too. Isn't a century alone enough for you?
The Entire Campus

Dear Entire Campus,
I know guys have feelings. That's why no third dates. If I know a guy is hopeless, why lead him on? Third dates that lead to fourth dates, and so on, only lead to that lovely state of mismatch everyone hates—that moment when you think you can change enough to make them love you. Or, if your psyche runs more along the lines of Freud, when you wonder how you can change them to fit your definition of perfect. A nightmare waiting to happen. And Mother Hubbard just happens to prefer to sleep well at night.

So let me sleep. E-mail Tyler at the

Campus Times, or at the e-mail I set
up: edgoneloco@ezeemail.com and
tell him to let Mother Hubbard off
the third-date train before someone
gets hurt.
Mother Hubbard

I sat back and looked at the column I
was going to try to get Tyler to run. He
hadn't backed down from his Hands-On-
Guy-or-further-public-humiliation threat.
But maybe he'd let the campus decide—
especially since he was the one who had
whipped them up into a frenzy.

I didn't miss that my decision to try to
break the stalemate was pure irony. In one
way, this should have been great—my best
chance to break for freedom, quit the column. Heck, maybe even quit classes. It was
too late to drop out and get my money
back (never mind explain to Mom and Dad
why I was home midsemester with nothing
to show for what was really their money),
but I still had time to withdraw without an
F on my permanent record. . . . Do they
have permanent records in college? I
haven't even been here long enough to find

out, and I'm already thinking of running away.

I thought maybe I could change roommates, or universities . . . take a semester—or four years—abroad. Far away from all this, surely I could get my life back to normal. . . . I could quit the column. And maybe I should quit the column. But I didn't want to. Not for any good, or even logical reason. All I knew was there was something stubborn inside me that refused to believe I would be better off transferring out of the university. Something that made me think maybe Tyler was a guy who could get me. If I could figure out this whole messy life thing. And not run away.

My thoughts of escape came to a grinding, screeching halt. Too much work. It would be easier to go on the date with Blaine than try to quit this job. I still had a point to make. And besides, quitting meant never seeing Tyler again. Irony that Shakespeare would envy, no doubt.

I'd thought college would be so very different—clarity after the murky life of high school, where all the fun things were forbidden and everyone who thought they knew the secret to life disagreed with one another. Some kids had the take-it-easy philosophy, some had the nose-to-the-grindstone mentality. And some, like me, just wanted to get out of high school and into college, where there would be no parents or teachers prying into our private lives every minute of the day.

I majored in mechanical engineering because it seemed so much more defined than my role in high school as the girl who liked math and hated gym. And the engineering and math classes were more clearly defined too. So much easier than all the eclectic general studies stuff they threw at us in high school. Read this, do these problem sets, learn this equation, and one day you will be an engineer. Crystal clear.

But college is about more than your major. There's still all the messy social stuff. There are just fewer rules to help navigate it all.

And therein lies the paradox. It is both the greatest and worst thing about college life. There are no adults to offer unsolicited advice about what you're wearing (or not wearing), whether you missed a class, or even if you stayed out past curfew. In fact, there is no curfew. However, the lack of rules or guidance doesn't make anything any clearer. There are still a million paths to take to "success."

And furthermore, what is success? A 4.0 GPA? A guy who gets you and likes you as much as you like him? Just managing to survive the four years and earn a piece of paper that might get you a job in the "real" world? Was the real world any better than high school or college? Do you ever in your life end up in a place where you have more answers than questions?

At least I had one answer to the column dilemma. I did not want to go out with Blaine for a third time. So I'd have to see if Tyler would go for my idea. As soon as he slid into the seat next to me in class, I slipped him the column, folded so no one sitting behind us could see it, of course. "Maybe we just let a third party arbitrate?"

He read the column surreptitiously and then ripped it into confetti and stuffed it in his pocket. I wasn't sure whether that was paranoia or commentary until he said,

"Maybe. But not in the column. We need to take this real time if we want to get it done by the end of the semester."

"Real time?"

"Yeah. I'm going to set up a blog on the paper's Web site. I'll put this in it and set up a vote for the campus."

"You will?" I wanted to protest this whole blogging in real time business, but I still hoped the campus would let me off. Wouldn't it be better to be let off the hook sooner rather than later? Spare myself these silly dates and get back to normal? "Okay."

"Great!" He looked at the sparse class turnout. "What's the topic for today?"

"AIDS." Sometimes I wondered if I was the only one who cared about good grades enough to actually study depressing subjects like AIDS, because the class was only full when the subject was something more stimulating, like kissing, birth control, and the factors of attraction.

"Good. I can take a miss, then, and get the blog up sooner. I'll catch your notes later."

He left. Which I suppose was better than Sophia, who had once again not shown up. That little shred of hope inside me woke up and whispered that Tyler hadn't even seemed to notice she wasn't there. So I ignored the louder whisper, which said he'd already confessed he'd thought about asking her out.

I had twenty-four blissful hours of hoping that I would not have to go on a third date with Hands-On Guy. After six hours the hope was a little bit against the odds. But still, I held out for a win for the home team until the bitter end.

Of course the campus voted overwhelmingly for me to go on the third date with Hands-On Guy. I compulsively checked the Web site for a while, but it never got better than two to one against me. The final tally was a whopping four to one against me. Or for the date, whichever way you choose to look at it. I preferred not to look at it.

Tyler seemed almost sympathetic when he delivered the bad news in person. He didn't even seem too disappointed that Sophia wasn't around. Although, I didn't miss that he checked out the closet, maybe thinking she might be hiding in there.

"Great. I give up. I'll go on the date with Hands-On Guy. Are you happy? I'll even pay for the stupid thing. And ask him out. And break all my usual rules for good dating."

"Ah! Rules for dating? You definitely should write a column about that."

"Okay. Should I also write about how much trouble I'm having in calculus and about how the freshman fifteen makes me feel like a pig?"

One more time he looked at me, really looked at me. "This is really hard for you, isn't it?"

"Well, duh! How would you like going out with girls you'd already written off?"

For a minute I thought he wasn't going to answer. But then, with a little laugh as if I shouldn't take him too seriously, he said, "Actually, after all this, I thought I might give it a try."

"What?" Shock doubled the buzz in my ears. "You're going to try it? For the column?" Did he mean he was going to write my column? And who cared about that. He was going to try dating a girl he hadn't given a chance before? Who?

"No." He shrugged. "For my life. Who knows. Maybe I just shot somebody down for some lame reason like I didn't like her hobby."

Now, on the one hand, I couldn't help hoping that I might be first on the list of girls he'd give a chance. On the other, I was a lot insulted. "What do you mean, lame excuse? Hobbies are something you have to put up with if you're going to be in a relationship. Even if you're going to be spending an evening together. I volunteered once for the torture of watching a stupid train movie for Todd, and I hated it. A lifetime of train movies would send me over the edge."

He held up his hands to calm me down. "Okay, okay. I'm not saying I'm looking for a girl who loves knitting so much I have to wear funny-looking sweaters and socks for the rest of my life. There's definitely a line. But maybe I'm crossing it too soon. That's all I'm saying."

I nodded, as if my ears weren't buzzing like there were flies trapped in them. *Don't, Katelyn,* I told myself silently, as my mouth disobeyed my brain. "Have you already decided on the first girl you'll ask?"

He squirmed in his seat. Was that a good sign or a bad one? "I don't want to say."

"Oh, come on, you know you're safe telling me." Well. He would be if he said it was me he wanted to take a chance on dating.

It only took that weak bit of reassurance to pry the name from his lips, which meant he was dying to tell someone. "Sophia."

For a minute the buzzing in my ears got so loud I hoped I'd heard wrong. But my eyes had been focused on his lips and the name was clear to even a bad lip-reader like me. Sophia. Of course.

I smiled widely. So widely it hurt. "Good luck." Not that I really wished him good luck. But I had to put on the best-friend front and pretend I did. Maybe I even would, after I got finished dealing with the disappointment that was flickering up and down my spine like a broken neon sign. Maybe I'd even be old maid of honor at their wedding.

What is it about me, anyway? Maybe every guy in the world only likes me as a best friend. Yep. That's it. I'm just better as a girl friend than a girlfriend. So why does that hurt so much? Why do I wish that— just once—I could find a boy who thought of me in the same way I thought of him?

I know that kind of relationship exists. I saw it every day in the high school hallways. I see it in college—in the dorms, on the benches outside the library. Not the classroom so much, although you can tell a couple like that when they walk in, just the way they are with each other, like they're restraining themselves from going at it out of respect for their professor (or fear of a failing grade).

Sometimes I think that guy doesn't exist for me. Even if my mother tells me I'll never find him if I don't give guys a chance. Which, I guess, is what Tyler and the others are trying to tell me too. Give a guy a chance, for crying out loud.

But the question I have for them is— how much of a chance? When is enough enough? How many hearts should I break to find the guy who gets me as much as I get him? Because I've had a broken heart, and, honestly, it ain't pretty.

Long story, short. The news was Tyler 1, me 0. Or maybe less than zero. Because Tyler changed the subject on me as I sat there reeling from the thought of Sophia and Tyler on a date.

"Katelyn. I just thought of something brilliant."

"What?" I didn't want to hear what Tyler thought was brilliant. The way college life has been going for me, it could be something off the wall, like that he'd decided to skip the dating stage altogether and just ask Sophia to marry him. And she'd agree. Bleh.

Fortunately, even my imagination was too absurd that time. "I want to make this Mother Hubbard third-date thing more immediate for the readers. I want them to have to come to our Web site on a consistent basis. The advertisers will love that."

"How?" I really didn't want to know the answer to that. But he told me anyway, in a tone of voice that told me he thought I ought to worship him for having the idea in the first place.

Tyler's big idea involved a lot of work—for me. In the blog on the paper's

Web site, between each week's column recapping the date, I was supposed to write about why I didn't think this guy had any shot at all at being the love of my life.

Oh joy. Joy, joy, joy. "Are you out of your mind, Tyler? We're keeping the date recaps generic, but if I start being specific, how long is that going to last?"

He waved away my objection. "You don't have to be specific specific."

"No? Just generally specific? Great."

"Try it. If I think there's any danger that the guy will recognize himself in your profile, I won't run it."

I wrote quickly on a napkin: *It won't work because this guy is looking for someone who likes the shell game. Or strip poker without a full deck. And I'm not a girl who likes to play a game I can't possibly win.*

He read it, laughed, and said, "Perfect."

Perfect. Sure. If you aren't the one who's going to have her life hijacked by Mother Hubbard.

Ten

Tyler got up to leave, with the napkin with my half-serious rant on it, and then stopped. He fished in his shirt pocket and came out with two tickets, which he handed to me.

"What are these?" I looked at them. Football. The homecoming game. Despite the fact that I was still recovering from his confession that he wanted to ask Sophia out, I immediately wondered if he was asking me out.

My heart even started to skip beats (Professor Golding explained in class that this was caused by excess adrenaline), until he said, "The paper always gets tickets to the president's box for homecoming. Take Hands-On Guy. That way you don't have to pay for the date."

"Thanks." I tried to inject some enthusiasm into my voice even though I hated football and had planned to skip the whole thing and enjoy how empty the gym was during a game—you could sign up for the elliptical machines without having to wait an hour.

The excess adrenaline slopping around inside me with nothing else to do apparently made me sound really happy, because Tyler stopped and looked at me for a second, halfway into standing up to leave. "No problem. If I'd known how much you loved football, I'd have offered sooner."

"Great." Again with the too much adrenaline. That must be the problem with perky people—they suffer from overadrenalitis. I took a sip of coffee, wondering whether that would make things better or worse. Perky and peppy was so not what I was going for right now.

Tyler, typical guy, was only aware of the perky, peppy stuff in his own editorial veins. "I'm going to post that Mother

Hubbard has agreed to go on third date number two. I'll advertise it in tonight's paper, too, so we can really get everyone paying attention to next week's issue with Mother Hubbard's column in it."

He held up the napkin I had scribbled on and then stuffed it in his pocket. "This will really get things going."

The way he said "things," I knew he meant "good things" like readership and ad revenues. I wasn't stupid enough to believe that. Just stupid enough to go out with Blaine. Because in my little pink book, Tyler had a buzz factor of ten.

Which is how I ended up in Sophia's hands . . . my own personal fashion fairy to help me go from best friend to femme fatale in a few shakes of a mascara wand.

She was also my cheerleader, since I desperately needed a pep talk before the "casual meeting" I had arranged in order to find a way to invite Blaine to the football game.

Sophia obliged with a smile, just before she disappeared with some cute hockey player. "You look like a woman who can invite a guy to a football game and leave him helpless to say no, Katelyn."

I was a little put out when I finally approached Blaine at the milk machine in the dining hall (which, I've learned, is a happening place when it comes to guys who take care of their bods . . . not that those guys don't go to the soda machine, just that the less health conscious don't bother with the milk).

I'd had to get six glasses of milk and hang out for an hour for that nonchalant, "Hi, how are you doing?" But I think I did it well, no sign of a milk mustache on *my* upper lip.

He said hi back. But there was no spark there. He was definitely sending air-conditioned vibes my way. I guess he still hadn't forgiven me for ditching the frat party. Of course, if it weren't for this stupid Mother Hubbard thing, I wouldn't be looking for another date either.

I backed off and considered giving up. But the thought of doing this again was a worse alternative than going through with the girl-asking-guy-out-on-a-date mission I'd accepted for the good of Mother

Hubbard, Tyler, and the entire campus.

Since he'd been very standoffish on my first greeting, I made sure to have the tickets visible when I approached again—filling my glass for the seventh time— "Hey, I have some box seat tickets for the homecoming game, and I was looking for someone to come with. You like football?"

The frost was receding as he took a sip of his chocolate milk, his eyes on the tickets, not on me. Sophia would not be pleased at the fashion fairy failure. "Who doesn't?"

Me. But I managed to keep that to myself because I knew instinctively that a guy who felt so strongly about his fraternity letters wasn't going to love my candid feelings on the silliness of a game where men wear skintight uniforms and run into one another in the pursuit of an oval of pigskin with no inherent value.

"So. Want to come?"

Like a WALK light that turns on when someone gets near, he lit up. "Wow. Football. A sunny day. A beautiful girl. How could I possibly resist?" Sudden. Abrupt, even. But, just like that, the magnet factor was as strong as the buzz factor. I was a little relieved I hadn't imagined the attraction between us last time. Don't get me wrong, I had a good idea it was the box at the football game that had won him over. Which didn't mean I wasn't glowing from the sudden attention from a very interested Blaine.

There was even a little relief underneath the glow. It never feels good to know you've alienated someone you thought you were clicking with. Who doesn't hate that nasty moment when the sparks start dying instead of flying? I had had no idea that a girl who wasn't appropriately reverential to the fraternity system was such a loser in his eyes.

Another part of me realized that it wasn't actually all that flattering that he'd turned on his magnetic charm after I'd flashed the tickets. Oh, well. There wasn't anything I could do about it.

When I finally was face-to-face—or should I say femme fatale to hot guy—with Blaine again for the official Third Date #2, I was surprised at the way his eyes got a little bigger and his smile lanterned on with no tickets in sight. "Katelyn, you're hot today." His focus, needless to say, was not on my face. Sophia, unhappy at my report of the fashion fairy failure at the milk machine, had convinced me to wear two garments that I am not normally in at the same time. A push-up bra and a low-cut top. Clearly, her magic had worked this time.

I doubt he had forgotten the football game, but there was no question that I (or my modest, but rather exposed, cleavage) had his attention. The way he turned "on" to me was an amazing sight—focusing on me, smiling, sending energy waves of interest. Which reminded me why I'd been worried about this date in the first place. I hadn't called him Hands-On Guy for nothing. He liked to touch.

On technical merit Third Date #2 actually started well. We met for coffee before heading for the game. We were both on time (well, Blaine was ten minutes late, but I already knew that could be considered on time for him). I had a double tall. It tasted good. But that was the last thing on the date that worked entirely as planned.

He didn't hold doors—yes, before anyone asks, I can open my own doors. But, I mean, he walked through every door in front of me and let it close behind him. I really hate swinging open a door that's already in the process of closing. Some of those pneumatic hinges really don't want to stop in the middle of a good close. I suppose the plus was that at least my arms got a good workout.

It turned out I was glad after all that Tyler had scored the football tickets. A football stadium was a very public place. With security. Because despite the lack of door holding, Blaine was definitely finding ways to make me feel like he was interested in me. I was a little uncomfortable at how easily I was sucked back in by his attention. Especially since I had already seen how quickly he could turn it on and off. But I liked the way he couldn't take his eyes off me. And I enjoyed feeling like a sexy date instead of a best-friend date.

He held my arm and touched my back and shoulder frequently, and at first it was great. If you had to go to a football game in the first place. The weather was sunny, not too cool. The guy was hot and definitely interested. The buzz factor was high. What could go wrong?

Where do I start? The nice thing about being in a box in the stadium is that you're covered. The bad thing is—you're covered. People can't really see in the boxes all that well (and why would they bother to crane around and look behind them when they came to watch the game?)

Fortunately, we weren't alone. Tyler had warned me that the president's box held a dozen people and was likely to be at least half full. At the homecoming game there were usually some bigwig alumni there that the president wanted to impress out of their money.

Besides the president, there were four men. In suits, so you knew they weren't there just to enjoy the game. Although, they stood up and shouted every time our team had the ball.

Blaine—after waiting a beat, which I later realized meant that he'd expected me to introduce him to the president and his guests—stuck out his hand and said, "Pleasure to meet you, sir, you run a tight campus."

The president seemed a bit surprised, but I had the tickets out, just in case anyone challenged us, so he shook Blaine's hand, introduced him to the alumni—all about eighty and ready to croak, as far as I could tell. For a second I had an unpleasant flash of Blaine sixty years from now, standing in line as one of the guys being primed for a mention of the university in the will.

We split up into age groups, the over fifty crowd on the left and the under twenty-one (Blaine and me), on the right. Near the food. Another good thing I should mention about being in the president's box is food. Real food. A couple of big round platters of cheese and crackers. Another one of fruit. And a cooler of drinks nestled in ice.

Blaine was very impressed. "This is great. How'd you score these tickets?"

I was feeling the moment—me hot in his eyes, the gorgeous day, the exclusive president's box, so I said without thinking, "The paper gets some perks."

He seemed a little shocked. "The paper? You work for the paper?" He said it loud enough that the president looked over for a moment.

"Umm." Great going, Katelyn. Why don't you get on the megaphone and just tell everyone you're Mother Hubbard. "Just this once. They needed someone to write up a story on the homecoming game."

"Do you like football?"

I could have said yes, but then he might have wondered why I'd closed my eyes during the last big rushing tackly move the opposing team did to get one over on our team. At least, as far as I could tell from the boos on our side of the stadium. "No. But there wasn't anyone else, and I didn't want to pass up free tickets."

"Really? I'd think there'd be lots of people who'd want to come to the homecoming football game."

I thought of the four people who'd been mad that Tyler had given me the tickets. "You'd think. But the regular sports person got sick suddenly, and I have a class with the editor, and . . . there you are." I leaned forward a little, using the cleavage Sophia had helped me showcase as a distraction. It was bad of me, but I was desperate to distract him from this topic before I got into real trouble.

"Good news for us, bad for him." Blaine took a soda out of the cooler and popped the top. "Want one?"

I took one, just for something to do. He sat down close to me, draped his arm around me, and squeezed me tight as he leaned in to pop my top.

He didn't move his arm, even after I took a nervous sip of my drink. My hand was shaking so hard I thought for sure I'd dump the contents of the can right into my cleavage zone. But I took tiny sips and avoided that humiliation.

Blaine was having no trouble adjusting to the relative luxury of watching football from a private box. He cheered when the running and jumping and kicking were good for us. And booed when they weren't. But he didn't let go of me while he did it.

When I felt his hand creep a little too far up under my shirt, I just moved it back down with a nod to the geriatric squad on our left. I'd been worried he might sulk at not getting his way, like he had before when we'd gone out. But he smiled and didn't protest, except to brush his lips against my ear and ask if I wanted more to drink.

I'm not sure I'd have said yes if I'd known Blaine was going to take a flask from his pocket and make the bland soda more interesting. But I may have anyway. There was a reason I'd given Blaine a top buzz factor. He tended to make everything sound like a great idea. He was the kind of guy who was used to hearing yes. When you were around him, you wanted to say yes.

By halftime I was ready to leave, but that wasn't an option. Blaine was still into the game, not to mention he'd think it was odd I was only going to report on half the game. Especially considering the score was close: 14–7. Not in our favor.

The cheerleaders and marching band were taking the field—and doing a good job.

So I pretended to be having a great time watching people run—or march—

around the field so he'd think I actually cared and wanted to see the end of the game.

All was good, until suddenly the geriatric brigade got noisy. I looked over to see what was up and caught the president's eye. He leaned over and whispered something. All I heard was "paper" but I could imagine the rest. The president has to put up with student newspaper reporters and their nosy questions because of the whole free speech thing. But he was still annoyed about the article that had been done on how, when he renovated the university's president's house, the furniture had been thrown out, or given to the workers. All the student groups were outraged that they didn't get to inherit some of the stuff. It didn't really mean anything, except that it made him look bad. Presidents don't like looking bad. It makes the board of trustees and the parents ask questions he doesn't want to answer.

Everyone looked over at our half of the box, and suddenly they shuffled out, the president saying, "In my office we can be more comfortable."

I watched them file out and thought about letting them know that I wasn't interested in exposing administrative or alumni secrets, I was just trying to have a nice little date. But I was pretty sure they weren't going to take my word for it.

"Great. I've got you to myself." Blaine pulled me closer and nuzzled my neck. His hand touched my bare back and stroked. He laughed when I jumped at the coolness of his hand. And I realized I didn't have the protection of the geriatric squad anymore. I was briefly worried. Briefly. But like I said, Blaine has a way of making things seem okay.

Eleven

I thought it was a good thing we were alone—with the food and the drinks and the game. Whatever was in Blaine's flask probably helped that warm buzz that I already had just from being the object of Blaine's affections.

Still, a little note of caution made me warn him, "They could be back any minute."

He laughed. "They're going across campus to the president's office. The speed they walk, it'll be an hour before they come back. If they come back. So don't worry."

Unusually enough, I didn't worry about the president of our university discovering us making out. Which was a good thing. Because we hadn't been alone for five minutes before we were making out. Not too heavy. Blaine still wanted to follow the game, and I had Mother Hubbard sitting on my shoulder, warning me that I was going to have to blog about this in the morning.

It was dark before we made our way back across campus. Blaine's arm was around my shoulders, which was nice. And warm. I had wondered, watching other couples wandering arm in arm, if it was awkward to walk that way. But it wasn't. It was nice.

"Let's sit here," he said, choosing a newer bench in front of the library.

I found my head rested just perfectly in the crook of his shoulder. It was a perfect moment. Unexpected, but considering how the date came about in the first place, a little humbling. I'd almost stopped wondering if I would do anything to make Blaine turn off the charm like he had last time. Maybe that was just a rare bad day. Besides, I really liked that he was keeping up with the warmies even after we'd made out. Sometimes a make-out session is just that. And when it's over, it's over. But this . . . whatever it was . . . was clearly not over for either of us.

I was almost ready to concede that maybe the students of the campus, who were breaking up and making up every minute of the day, were right and Mother Hubbard was wrong. Just maybe this random hooking up does eventually lead to a real relationship. Maybe there didn't need to be rules about when to stop trying to make a connection. Maybe.

We were, for a moment, so comfortable that we didn't even need to talk. I had been in this place only once before—and not with a boyfriend, but with a boy friend. David. Who was on another coast, at another university, and with another girl.

To be here, with Blaine on a college campus—no parents in sight—dressed like a girlfriend, treated like a girlfriend . . . there weren't really any words. So I enjoyed the silence and Blaine's arm around me.

"What are you thinking?"

I turned toward him instinctively at the question and he kissed me. It was a good kiss. Warm and not too slobbery. I knew what I liked. And I liked knowing that Blaine wanted to kiss me, even after our heavy-duty make-out session at the football game.

Things were going well until I noticed that Blaine's hand was under my shirt again, warm on my back.

It felt good, so even though I knew there was a good reason I should ask him to move it, I couldn't remember what it was. Until I heard a giggle. Not Blaine (thank goodness). Not me. Just some random girl walking by. About a foot away from where we were making out in public, dark or not.

I pulled away. "Hey. Not here." I was thinking that maybe my room would be a good choice, but he didn't give me a chance to make the offer.

"It's better with a little risk." He pulled me closer again, totally missing that I was no longer in the mood. Which really got me out of the mood. Completely.

"Not here, Blaine." I once again tried to extricate myself. And couldn't. He'd wedged me against the back of the bench and I couldn't move.

Now. One thing about me that I don't like to publicize is that I'm claustrophobic. When I was three I locked myself in my closet (way too packed with cute little dresses and some of my mom's stuff she wasn't wearing anymore). Mom didn't hear me for two hours.

I don't do locked in closets—or locked in unbreakable embraces, either. So it was panic time when Blaine wouldn't let me go, even if he was being more charming than scary.

The karate class from long ago came back to me. I slipped the tight hold Blaine had on me and slid into the bed of white stones that surrounded the bench. "Enough. Not here."

He grabbed his elbow in pain. Apparently, I'd twisted it harder than I thought, when I Houdini'd out of his hold. "What the hell is wrong with you?" The look on his face reminded me of when I'd joked about the name of his fraternity. Only worse.

I sat there on the ground, feeling ridiculous. Fortunately, no one happened by and the windows of the library remained empty of curious faces. "I said no. Didn't you hear me? I don't like making out in public." I guess I still had a little panic left, because my voice sounded angry. But I was a little numb from panic and embarrassment, so who knows.

Blaine watched me with a chilly frown for half a second, and then his charm turned right back on as he reached out a hand. "A little shy, are you?"

I took his hand and let him pull me up. Mistake.

He pulled me into his lap and held on tight. "Maybe you just haven't taken the risk with the right guy."

So. The panic came back. And this time some real anger. I mean, how much more "no" did he need? I socked him hard enough that he let me go.

Then I ran.

What can I say? I'm not used to guys kissing me in public, and I'm not proud of having a claustrophobic meltdown in the middle of hooking up. But I was feeling some shady vibes, so panic took over and it didn't intend to let go until I had run myself out. Probably a good thing.

"Katelyn! Wait!" I heard running behind me. Naturally, I ran faster, despite the fact that everything, in the darkness, looked unfamiliar. I felt like a girl who'd accidentally wandered into one of those stalker movies. Which wasn't the best thing for someone who was already acting out of sheer panic.

Just as I realized he was gaining on me, I turned a blind corner and found myself in a familiar part of campus. It wasn't any better lit than the rest of campus, but there was a light on in a window. It was put the paper to bed night, I remembered, ducking quickly through the door, in too much of a hurry to be quiet, so the door slamming shut echoed in a not so good way.

I found Tyler and Sookie bent over a page layout dilemma. They had straightened up when I came in and slammed the door shut behind me breathlessly. They said nothing for a moment after I turned the lock. I didn't have enough breath after all that running to say anything either.

Tyler looked me up and down. "Hot date?" For a minute I wondered why he was looking at me as if he'd never seen me before. Then I remembered that I was dressed like a girl on a date instead of in my usual best-friend uniform of sweater and jeans.

I looked down to check to make sure nothing was showing that shouldn't be. Nope. Luck was with me and I hadn't pelted across campus in a panic with my pushed-up self popped out of my low-cut hot girl top. There was maybe a little action going on since I was still struggling to catch my breath, but nothing a hot girl should be ashamed of. Sophia would be so proud. Grace under fire, that's me.

Tyler may not have had a clue about the situation code red, but Sookie didn't even hesitate. "Hands-On Guy lived up to his name, huh? Is he right behind you?"

I gasped, "I think I might have lost him."

Right. Just then the doorknob by my hip jiggled. "Katelyn?" A knock. "Let me in. Did you get stung by a bee or something?"

I just stood there, looking at Tyler, wondering what he thought about all this.

Stung by a bee? At night? Well, no,

Blaine, I didn't. I wish I had, though. That might help explain my crazy run across campus in a more flattering way than the truth did. I wanted to die. Or at least melt away like ice girl meets flame boy, into a steaming puddle of shame.

"You're not here." Sookie whispered. A command, not a question, as she shoved me away from the door and toward a tiny storage closet. For the first time I appreciated all the benefits of a Lois Lane approach to life.

Until I saw the closet. Tiny. Full of junk. I dug my heels in and all thought stopped.

"Get in." She pushed me forward, ignoring my reluctance. There was room for me to crouch down and hide. But not much.

The door handle jiggled again. "Katelyn! I know you're in there."

Even my claustrophobia wasn't enough to protest. A musty stuffed stationery closet looked good to me—better than facing Blaine, anyway.

I pressed my ear to the door and pretended I was in a suite at the Ritz Carlton.

A suite with a door that was flaking off paint and greasy with grime from who knows how many years.

After a few shufflings and a quick command from Sookie to Tyler, I heard Blaine's voice. "Did you see a girl come in here?"

As I sat sweating in the dark, listening and trying to pretend I wasn't stuck in a dark, musty closet, Sookie lied without a flicker of hesitation. "Nope. Just us editor types putting the paper to bed."

Blaine sounded like he was slowly getting his charm back after his mad dash across campus behind me. "I know I saw a girl run in here. I just want to—"

"The only girl here is Sookie." Tyler sounded a little on the growly side. Good. That meant he wouldn't be charmed into telling Blaine what he wanted to know.

I listened for the sound of Blaine leaving. The closet was hot. And there was a box of pencils stuck in my back. Did I mention how tiny the closet was? I could tell even in the dark. Which was very dark.

"I—"

Sookie interrupted whatever Blaine was going to say with a laugh, and for a minute

I was afraid Blaine had charmed her with his smile. I should have known better. "There isn't any woman here but me. But if you're desperate, I'm available."

To my great relief, Blaine believed her and left just before my claustrophobia sent me out of the closet in a tsunami of paper and pencils. I looked over my shoulder, wondering if I could bear to put everything back as long as I left the door open.

Tyler locked the door, turned to look at me on the floor with office supplies surrounding me, and just shrugged. He rolled a chair across the room to me and said, "Sit. I'll get that later. What just happened here?"

Sookie looked at him with the scorn he full well deserved. She waved her cigarette pack under my nose. "Date didn't go well?"

I declined the offer with a wave, and climbed into the chair like I hadn't just clawed my way out of a closet. It was a feat, but I think I managed to make my voice sound normal, almost joking, when I said, "Sure it did. It's just over."

Tyler paced, as if he were trying to figure out how to edit down a headline to fit and grab attention at the same time. The ADD Thinker look again, if the Thinker got up from his marble seat and paced. "What did he do? Do you want me to go after him?"

"Nothing. He didn't do anything." Which wasn't completely true. He hadn't listened when I said no. Still, he'd just held me on his lap. And I'd punched him. I'd never hit someone like that before.

"So I guess the red mark on his cheek was just your way of saying you had a nice time at the football game?" Tyler sat down and looked at me. Really looked at me. "I'm glad you clocked him." He gestured at my chest. "You look nice, except for that."

For a minute I thought he was saying I wasn't well endowed enough, and I thought about clocking him for the insult. But then I looked down. I had a pink Post-it note stuck in my cleavage that said "While You Were Out."

"Thanks." I took out the pad and tossed it to him. I was too tired out from two panic attacks in a row to care. "Sophia dressed me—though I don't think she'd approve of that accessory."

Sookie laughed. "She has taste—too much if we go by Just Say No Guy."

"Yeah. Just Say No Guy. That suits him even better than Hands-On Guy."

"While you're here, why don't you write your column." Tyler put his laptop in front of me.

Sookie raised an eyebrow, but Tyler just said, "What? I'm going to walk her home, and I have to get one more thing done here before we go. She may as well get it down while it's fresh in her memory." He looked at me, and I could tell he got how much I wanted to erase what just happened. "Then she can forget it. Hands-On Guy is history."

"Ancient history," I agreed. As long as I found another dining hall to eat in.

So, Third Date #2 was fun. If you like guys with eight hands who don't get the meaning of "no."

I felt a little weird writing about my experience. How much to say? How much to leave out? I ended up not saying much—I had to leave out football and the president's box, and even the exact location of the make-out session gone wrong. I may even have made it all seem a lot worse than it was, because I was writing on the left-over adrenaline from my panic attack and the caffeine from the rest of Tyler's large latte. But I think I captured the true nature of the encounter. Because the entire campus was buzzing about it the day the paper hit the stands in the student union.

The consensus seemed to be either (a) I was a tease, or (b) Hands-On Guy should become Hands-Off Guy the hard way. I was starting to wonder if anyone ever bothered to take the middle ground anymore.

It may have been weird to write about my experience, but what was getting even weirder was hearing people talking about it on campus and not being able to say anything to defend myself.

Not to mention the comments I was getting on the blog, and in the Mother Hubbard e-mail—Tyler had had to set up a separate one for the column because he'd lost track of an ad request in all the e-mail about Mother Hubbard.

One particular e-mailer, named

Anonymously_Yours, had started out by echoing my own thoughts pretty closely. I'd begun to recognize his posts and think of him as a possibility in the huge pool of college guys around me. After this Mother Hubbard experiment was over, of course. If he ever decided to reveal his identity, of course.

> Do you ever wonder if anyone will ever love you as much as you love . . . him . . . ? What if someone did, but you didn't know who he was?

> If you fall in love in the forest, with only the trees to hear, are you really in love?

But then, after the column about my date with Hands-On Guy, there was one e-mail from Anonymously_Yours that made me stop and reread it, three times. Each time I got more creeped out.

> You deserve to be loved for the wonderful person you are. The

smart, funny girl who likes strawberry milk and cell phone roulette.
Why don't you look for love where
you've missed it before?

Nothing major at first glance, but I
finally realized what was creeping me out
on the third read. How did this guy (or
girl, I guess) know I liked strawberry milk?
I didn't drink it in the dining hall. They
only had chocolate.

In fact, I hadn't had strawberry milk
since I'd come to campus. I'd asked my
mom to send me a bottle of strawberry
syrup because I couldn't find it in the stores
around here—but she hadn't sent it yet
because she's care package challenged.

No surprise, that. I'd learned that long
ago when I went away to Girl Scout camp
and came home to find three packages
she'd meant to send me but hadn't (not to
worry, the candy and cookies were still
good—plus I didn't have to share, except
with my little brother).

No worries. I'd figured I'd get a bottle
from home when I went back for break.
The way the dining hall made me pack on

the pounds, I didn't need the extra calories, anyway. Which didn't tell me a thing about who knew of my strawberry milk craving.

I printed out the e-mail, thinking I'd ask Tyler if there was a way to find out who'd sent it. Maybe it was someone I knew. Or maybe it was some crazy stalker. Great. Just what I needed.

Twelve

Professors always like to throw curveballs in class. I suppose it comes from being forced to teach the same material over and over again to—overall—people who just want the class to be about what grade they can skim off, not the actual knowledge. I mean, how often am I going to use calculus in my regular life?

Now, Professor Golding is luckier, I suppose, in that she has a naturally . . . sexy . . . subject. But she still likes to throw us curveballs every now and then.

"I've been following the Mother Hubbard columns closely these past three weeks, and I have to commend you, Tyler, for finding a new way to explore what makes a relationship blossom and what stops it."

Tyler stood up. Modest he is not. "What I like about this campus is how everyone seems to be participating. I hear people talking about us everywhere I go."

Right. And even some places he doesn't go. Like the ladies' rooms between classes. Part of me wants to stand up. Not a good idea, because I want to scream, "What about me? I have to live it!"

Professor Golding keeps going. "I think Mother Hubbard struck a blow on behalf of all women when she insisted that her date take no as an answer, even though he was more used to hearing yes. Rape is an ugly thing."

Tyler turned red and stammered. "She wasn't—"

"Of course not. Because she got herself out of an uncomfortable situation before things could get out of hand." Professor Golding beamed at the class, and Tyler sat back down and gave a little sigh at being out of the unexpected line of fire. "She trusted her instincts. And that's what we're going to talk about today. Instincts when it comes to love—or what may not be love at all."

I spent about ten seconds feeling like I was the smartest girl in the world for trusting my own instincts, even though they had led me directly into humiliation. Then it suddenly dawned on me that this wasn't a throwaway comment for Professor Golding. No. This was part of the lesson plan. As I recalled from the syllabus, the topic was "When Love Goes Wrong: Rape, Incest, and Abuse."

My timing was impeccable. Apparently, Mother Hubbard's ungodly journey into third dating is going to be used as a shining example. Oh, goody.

Professor Golding walked to the board and picked up the chalk. "We've already talked about what makes one person attractive to another. Anyone want to remind us?"

One guy—Joker Boy, I'd come to think of him—called out, "A shower."

The class laughed. Even the professor smiled as she wrote "shower" down on the board.

"That's one thing—in our culture. Which is interesting because the chemistry of attraction is correlated with our senses of smell and sight."

"Don't forget taste." Joker Boy was on a roll.

Professor Golding didn't even frown at him. I guess she might have appreciated someone who could lighten the mood. Our subject matter for the class was likely to make us all tense. "Not everyone gets to that stage before the senses of sight and smell have turned us away."

"Maybe that's Mother Hubbard's problem—she doesn't have a sense of smell." A guy way in the back in a torn T-shirt and a bored expression called out.

Joker Boy didn't like losing his momentum. "Right on. Mother Hubbard says she even turns the hotties away. What else could explain that?"

A girl who looked like she'd spent six hours getting ready for class, her hair was so model perfect, said skeptically, "Maybe she's lying. No one turns hotties away."

One poor clueless guy shouted, "There aren't guy hotties, anyway."

The girls in the class let out a collective belly laugh at that one, and the decidedly not hot speaker turned red with embarrassment.

"The question remains, how many of you have turned someone away for a reason that was changeable? If you'd stuck it out, would it have lasted? Or were your instincts worth trusting?"

I raised my hand. What can I say? There weren't a lot of freshmen in the class, and I didn't have too much experience with just speaking out. But I was tired of not having an opinion on the subject just because I was the opinion behind Mother Hubbard.

Professor Golding looked at me, taking me in, like she did all her students who contributed during class. I only had one second to worry that I'd been unwise to speak up before she said, "Yes, Katelyn, is it?"

Too late. I couldn't back out now, or she'd think I was lame. Who knew what that would do to my grade. "What if love takes time to develop, but it's better that way, instead of just letting your nose lead you?"

She nodded, and smiled as if she knew just what I meant. "Ah! Slow and steady, building up a fire from nothing but kindling, a small spark and a lot of time?"

I nodded.

"I call that the best-friends approach, and it is definitely one way for a relationship to grow. Good question."

"That's a crock!" The guy in the torn T-shirt was definitely hostile to the discussion today—and we hadn't even got to the hard part yet. Professor Golding was just easing us into it. "That's just something best friends tell themselves to keep from crying themselves to sleep at night."

"Whoa. Sounds as harsh as Mother Hubbard."

Everyone turned to look at T-shirt Guy, but then shook their heads. He was clearly an upperclassman, and had a beer gut to prove it. Older students were usually more cynical. Although, this guy was a harder case than the others I'd seen. Probably to compensate for the fact that he was already starting to lose his hair. Which the professor had pointed out was a sign of high testosterone.

I pretended I was turned to listen to what he had to say, when really I was examining him. Not a hottie. Probably never had been, even when he had hair. But the high testosterone and the muscles made me think he didn't have trouble hooking up. Getting to the third date may not have been working for him, though. Did the testosterone make him smell better or worse to women? Or was there something else that made him cynical?

Joker Boy didn't like losing the attention to T-shirt Guy. "I don't care how a girl smells if I like how she looks."

Professor Golding dismissed his comment with a quick smile. "You're not the first young man to declare that sentiment, but blind studies prove you're in the minority, if you're right about your own preferences." The class erupted into commentary at that.

"Isn't it called love at first sight? Not love at first smell? And what about the billion-dollar business in makeup? I bet if we asked every girl in here to hold up their makeup, we'd have hundreds of dollars' worth."

"Hey—don't forget the perfume and scented soap and lotion business. That's catering to the sense of smell."

"And scented candles on dates."

Joker Boy tried to hold his own against the majority of the class. "That's to hide the fact you haven't cleaned your apartment in a month, not that you haven't showered."

"Don't forget the smell of food—my mother always says the way to a man's heart is through his stomach."

Professor Golding broke in. "Interesting discussion. We're a little off topic, but before we get back to the subject on the syllabus for today, I have a question for you. Do any of you think you 'missed' the love of your life because you didn't give someone enough of a chance?"

"No way. One chance. That's all any of us get."

"I'd like to challenge us all to a general experiment." There was a collective groan at the thought of extra work.

"For extra credit." The groan softened.

I wrote down the assignment, just like everyone else, even though I was fuming inside at the unfairness of it all. Blogging for Mother Hubbard had seriously cut into my study time. Extra credit was going to be a real stretch.

"Anyone who gives a second chance to someone they've written off, then writes a three-page paper on the results —confirmation of attraction or not— gets an A on the chapter quiz, and doesn't have to take it either.

Hmmm. That was an appealing thought—at least to those of us who thought knocking out a three-page paper was nothing. Except I was already doing the work. I'd already done it twice over. And I couldn't claim it. Because then Professor Golding would know I was Mother Hubbard. Sigh.

I was almost relieved when we got back to the subject on the syllabus. The upshot was, trust your instincts and run, even if you look silly. Don't let anyone make you do what you don't want to do. And don't make excuses for bad behavior. Not even if you're really Mother Hubbard and have to sit there listening to people talk about you without knowing who you are.

Dear Mother Hubbard,
There's a girl I like. She talks to me,
but I don't know if she'd agree to go
out with me, so I don't ask.
Don't Shoot Me Down

Dear Don't Shoot,
Ask her. Otherwise you're wasting
your time wondering and not moving on. If she says yes, you're a stud.
If she says no, try a six-pack and let
the hangover wipe her from your
mind so you can try again.

Think about it. If she doesn't get
how wonderful you are, why would
you want her, anyway?
Mother Hubbard

I typed the last sentence with a little
jolt. It was sound advice. So why couldn't I
follow it? Had I passed up a person I could
love—who would love me back—just
because I let my crush make me too picky?
I thought about the guys I'd gone out with
in high school and my first weeks of college.

Were the readers right that I'd invented

reasons not to go on a third date? Was longing for the clarity of those old-fashioned dating rules actually just keeping me from finding someone? No. I refused to believe that. After all, I'd given every guy a second chance. What more could a girl do?

No. I just hadn't been lucky at the dating game yet. But that didn't mean the odds weren't with me . . . did it? I had to believe that, at some point in the near future, I'd find a guy worthy of a third date. Otherwise known on campus by the code name "the one."

The one. I hadn't used that phrase so much in . . . forever. But I was using it a lot in my blog. Besides being gender neutral, "the one" just sounded better than "Mr. Right." Because there is no such thing as Mr. Right. There's only the one whose shortcomings you don't mind because he makes you overlook your own imperfections.

There's something so appealing about blogging. It seems like just you and your keyboard and screen. Dear Diary, with the lock and key that your little brother always wants to steal and all that.

And the comments are as addictive as potato chips. You can't read just one.

When I blogged about Hands-On Guy being so cute that I was afraid I'd do something I'd regret in the morning (who knew I was a prophet?), I got these kinds of replies—from very different types of people:

> Grow up. Life is a risk. That moment you're afraid you'll regret in the morning could be the one instant you'll remember fondly forever—remember *Bridges of Madison County*?

Well, frankly, no. I had heard about it. It was a book. Maybe a movie. Some old guy fooling around with a farmer's wife. There was probably even a bridge in there somewhere, but I didn't see how that applied to my situation. And, as it turned out, my risk with Blaine had been riskier than I'd expected. And now I had to do it all over again.

I confess I had some hope that, after the exciting times with Blaine, the bloggers would vote to let me out of the third-date hamster wheel. No such luck. More people thought like the *Bridges of Madison County* guy than like the smarter bloggers—especially the smartest one, who had come right out and said:

> You're right to be cautious, MH. I wasn't quite so cautious and now I'm paying the price. I have to sit in class and watch the one I love sharing his notes, and his potato chips, with *her*. How can anyone be expected to learn physics under such terrible circumstances?

Now, that girl I could relate to. She and I both knew it was no fun to love someone who just didn't know you existed and had the bad taste to be happy within sight of you.

So caution was the watchword of Mother Hubbard—and her alter ego, Katelyn. Too bad it sometimes backfired.

Thirteen

Tyler came to pick up my column in the dorm. He was becoming such a fixture, I was getting teased about my "boyfriend." I tried to leave everything a mystery on that front—the last thing either of us wanted was for anyone to get curious about why he was coming over so often.

He sat down and watched me blog for a while. "You're good at this."

"It's not hard to give advice, it's only hard to take it." I sensed there was something on his mind and he didn't know how to approach it. But I wasn't in the mood to make things easy for him.

Finally, after he'd spent several minutes

fiddling with my desk lamp so that the shade was now crooked, he said, "I'm having second thoughts about this third date of yours."

Hallelujah! But I was cautious. Maybe he didn't mean what I hoped he meant. "You not only want to pick him, you want me to marry him, just to see if it really can work out?"

"No." He knocked over the lamp and quickly set it upright. "Not exactly. It's just . . . After class, I was thinking . . ."

Color me foolish, but I was hoping he'd tell me to forget it. That two third dates were enough. That even if the students on campus didn't care about my safety, he did.

What can I say? Hope sprang eternal, until he said, "I think we should double-date for the next one."

"Double-date?" I parroted what he said, but it was so far from what I had expected that it took a minute to process. Double-date? Me and . . . some guy. Tyler and . . . some girl? Was he kidding?

"It would be perfect. You'll be safe from any guy who isn't so great at hearing no. Plus, it will keep the cover—you won't report it as a double date, so we'll throw off anyone who's suspicious."

"I guess." I was trying to imagine whether a double date with Tyler would be better than going out alone with a guy I hadn't wanted to see again in the first place. Or much worse. I was coming down on the side of much worse.

He still seemed a little nervous. I wondered what else he wanted. After a while he said casually, "Do you think Sophia would be a good fourth? That way you'll have two friends to back you up."

And he'd have his date with Sophia without having to put himself on the line. Sweet. For him. "I don't know. You'll have to ask her."

"Okay. If she doesn't want to, I can ask someone else." I was a little touched that he wanted to protect me enough to go through with the suggestion even if Sophia turned him down. And a little peeved that he wanted to use a double date to get me to get Sophia to date him. I definitely wasn't going to do his work for him.

To my semi-chagrin, Sophia came back early from the party she'd been at—

evidently her hottie du jour had a game the next day and was under coach's orders to avoid alcohol and late-night fun. She didn't seem all that upset when Tyler asked her about double-dating—with heavy emphasis on protecting me from an unknown guy, of course.

She immediately agreed. "Ever since Professor Golding's challenge, I've been meaning to try dating someone I wouldn't normally date," she confessed to us both. "This sounds like it will be a good place to start."

"Then all we need is the guy for my half of the double date." I couldn't help but be pleased to hear she only considered him a start. But still, they were dating each other, and I was stuck with—who was I stuck with?

Of course, I wasn't so pleased at the third—and thankfully final—date that Tyler picked out for me (I'd tried to convince him that I could choose, but he wasn't about to let that happen).

His fickle finger of fate had fallen on Space Cadet, otherwise known as Stephen. A nice guy who liked robots. And wasn't too sure about girls . . . not that he was gay. Just not sure that he wanted to spend the time away from his robots that a girlfriend would require.

We'd met at the university museum, which was exhibiting video games dating back to Pong. (Who'd want to spend hours batting a ball of light around a black screen? All the geeks who jammed the exhibit.) I was there doing extra credit for a class, he was there because . . . well, he wanted to be. He'd earned solid scores in listening as the museum docent gave a spiel on every game exhibited. All fifty.

Unfortunately, he dressed like he'd just pulled the clothes out of his dryer, where they'd been sitting for a week. And he lost ten points on the talking front, since aside from one five-minute gush about how much the game Frogger had meant to him as a kid, he stuck to hello, yes, and no.

I guess it's obvious that his buzz factor was low—but don't blame me, the guy not only didn't have a car, he didn't have a driver's license. He didn't see the need, since he intended to invent a car that drove itself. O-kay.

I'm not exactly sure why I hung out with him the first time. Maybe because I didn't want to look like a loser next to Sophia, who sometimes had more than one guy to keep her occupied on a Saturday evening. But the second date with Stephen was pure pity. He asked me to a talk on robotics by some famous guy I'd never heard of before. On the plus side, he bought ice-cream cones after the talk and walked me to the dorm, but he didn't even try for a kiss.

I was happy about the double date idea, even though I didn't have any worries about Stephen in the "just say no" department. He had very limited interests and he was polite to a fault. I think the first time he'd asked me out, he'd been as surprised as I was that he'd even asked.

With Tyler and Sophia around, there would be actual conversation about a subject that interested me. And Tyler liked computer games, so Stephen would have someone who would understand what he was talking about too.

The only problem was how to ask him out. We didn't have any classes together.

We had met in line at the museum, waiting for the tour to begin. I didn't have his cell number—and yes, he did have a cell phone. I guess the gadget thing convinced him it was worthwhile, even if he did mostly use it to send pictures of his robots in progress back to his parents.

And e-mail just didn't feel right. What if he said no? It would be bad enough to be rejected for a third date by Stephen, but even worse if it happened in a one-word—no—e-mail.

I decided to stake out the student union because I knew Stephen liked the convenience store there. He spent so much time in his lab with his robots that he often forgot to eat during regular dining hall hours and needed to run out to get a big bag of chips and some cupcakes to sustain his late-night work.

While I was busy stalking Stephen, I'd forgotten to watch my back. So I nearly jumped to the ceiling when someone came up behind me and said, "Hi, Katelyn."

I turned around, half expecting that Stephen had read my mind and come up to me instead of my having to find him.

Sometimes life really is that whacked. But not tonight. It was Richie. The guy who had had a crush on me in high school.

"Hi, Richie." I hoped I didn't sound as unenthusiastic as I felt. I was stressing big-time over Stephen and the whole double-dating thing. I just didn't have the energy to put a fake happy smile on.

"I'm glad I ran into you." He didn't seem to mind that I didn't feel the same way. But then, he probably had gotten used to that in high school. "I'm in the play this weekend, and I was thinking you might want to come see it and then go get something to eat after?"

Great. Just what I needed. He'd finally found the nerve to ask me out, and I'd been too busy stressing to stop him before the words were out there.

Now here they were, hanging between us like a big sticky spiderweb of complications. So now what? Did I give yet another excuse? I could always tell him I had plans; it would be true as soon as I ran into Stephen.

Or did I rip the Band-Aid off, no matter how much it would hurt him?

Professor Golding's assignment tempted me for a moment. What if I just gave in and agreed to date him? Once. One little date. What could it hurt? I knew the answer to that—him. Richie deserved better than that. He was a great guy, but he was not for me and I didn't need even one date to know that. I'd known him since childhood.

I'm just not interested in you that way. I thought about how to soften those words. Like it was possible. I remember when David said them to me when he asked me to the prom. "Will you go to the prom with me, Katelyn? Please. Just friends."

Since I was his best friend—yeah, right—he went on to explain his dilemma. "I tried to explain to Celine that I just don't feel the same way about her as she does about me, but she doesn't get it. She thinks that just because we were an item for a nanosecond, I can't be telling the truth when I say there's nothing. And I mean nothing—no spark. I like her well enough, but like a sister. Like you. You know what I mean?"

What could I say? I did know what he meant. Man, did that hurt. And yes, I did go to the prom with David, and I sat at the table while he danced with several cute girls who, apparently, did spark with him.

Not only that, but I wished him well when he went home with one of those girls. Like a good best friend, he dropped me off at home before they went out to . . . whatever. That was us, very good friends. But I'm doing my best to graduate from best-friend status just like I've graduated from high school.

If only Richie had gone to a West Coast university like David, and wasn't standing in front of me, looking so completely breakable. I think he might even have been holding his breath, waiting for the answer I wasn't sure how to give.

"I don't feel that way about you. I like you as a friend. But there's no spark." Apparently, I'd decided on the Band-Aid method. Rip, rip, rip.

Richie stood there for a minute, a big, very fake smile growing on his face. Since he was a relatively good actor, I had no illusions about how much my rejection had hurt him. And then he said stiffly, "I understand, I just had to ask. Mother Hubbard said—"

"Mother Hubbard?! I didn't mean—I mean, she didn't mean—" Oh, crappinetta. I'd actually told this guy to come up and get the skin and hair ripped off his ego? Or, at least my know-it-all persona had.

After a minute of silently staring at each other in horror at how things had gotten way awkward way fast, I finally squeaked out, "Mother Hubbard doesn't always know what she's talking about. Or haven't you heard the vocal opinions of the rest of the campus?"

"I just hoped—" And by the look in his eyes, he was still holding on to a crumb of hope.

So I interrupted him. "I know." I don't know what turned me into confessing Katelyn, but I said, "I've been there. Do you know I had the biggest crush on David all four years of high school? He never looked at me as more than a friend."

Richie looked surprised. "He took you to the prom, didn't he?"

"And danced half the night with Patty Holloway. In fact"—I'd never confessed this to anyone, not even my mom when she asked why I was so cranky after prom—

"He went out with her afterward, too."

"Ouch." It was a miracle. My confession made his smile dim, but now it was a more genuine smile instead of a "I'll die before I let her see how hurt I am" grin. I remembered that was what I always liked about Richie. He really liked people and took them as they were. It wasn't his fault he'd had the bad fortune to crush on me. Or mine, either—neither one of us could control our pheromones after all.

I shrugged. "You're a really nice guy. There's somebody out there for you, I'm sure. Me? I'm not so sure. I went from lusting after David to wanting a junior who suggested we double-date—with other people!"

"Double ouch." He grinned for real— but I knew it was because he shared my pain, and was just acknowledging that life was like that. "Hey, if you find a girl for me, let me know."

"Only if you promise to do the same for me."

He went for the joke, and I'll always love him a little bit for it. "So you're into girls, too?"

I couldn't help laughing. What can I say? It was better than crying. "Funny guy. I meant if you find a guy for me, point him out."

He nodded and with a look of surprise, started fishing in his shirt pocket.

"Don't tell me you have a guy in there?" Lame, I know. But besides having to deal with letting Richie down easily, I also had one eye peeled to catch Stephen if he should come in for a munchie run.

He pulled out tickets. "Nope, just tickets to our production of *A Midsummer Night's Dream.*

I waved my hands, refusing the tickets. "No, I—"

He smiled. "I think you should go— especially if your crush really suggested you double-date with other people. The plot is a little closer to your life right now than you probably remember from high school when Mr. Jamison taught it to us."

"Right." Like I understood it in high school. That was one confusing play. And the names were even more confusing. Hermia? Puck?

"Seriously," he said, and I could tell he

meant it. "We have trouble filling the seats. They give us these tickets to give out to our friends so we'll have an audience to play to."

"So you were asking me out in desperation for an audience?" I joked without thinking.

The last little shreds of hope showed themselves in his face. "After was where I thought we could make it special." He recovered, though, and added, "Besides, I wanted to impress you with my skill at handling my little part in the play."

"If you put it that way. How can I refuse?" Awkward, I know. But what could I do? Since he wasn't going to leave until I took the tickets, I reached for them. "Thanks."

He held on to them for a minute and looked right into my eyes. It was way weird, because I thought I saw him deliberately crush out the last hope that I'd ever feel about him the way he felt about me. Freaky. "I also think you should take that junior guy with you."

"I don't know if I'm as brave as you." To be honest, until that very second when I'd watched him conquer his crush, I had only intended to drop the tickets on a chair in the student union lounge for someone else to use.

But Richie had reminded me that I needed something to do this weekend. And if I used these tickets, I could do Richie and the theater department two favors. I could provide four people for the audience. And I could make Tyler—or the paper—spring for two more tickets. Minor revenge and minor reparation, at the same time.

He shook his head and left me with this parting shot. "Better the Band-Aid method, like you used with me—and you never know, you might be surprised. Mother Hubbard might have been right. Girls who like strawberry milk may charm a clueless crush, if they give it a chance."

Strawberry milk. I looked into his eyes. Did he know I was Mother Hubbard? I'd forgotten I'd mentioned the strawberry milk in one of my very first columns. So, no stalker, just a secret admirer who liked girls who liked strawberry milk. Just Richie. He smiled at me, but I couldn't tell if he'd put two and two together and got Katelyn equals Mother Hubbard. I smiled back, and as he turned to walk away, I was almost tempted to ask. But if I did, then he would know. He was no dummy. And really, I wasn't the only girl on campus who liked strawberry milk.

The room felt about ten degrees cooler after he walked away, and I realized I'd been sweating. So had he, judging by the little stain on his shirt at the small of his back. Ain't misaimed love grand?

So maybe he knew my secret and maybe he didn't, but I definitely knew his. Although, come to think of it, if he'd come right out and told me he wanted to go out with me, was it a secret anymore? Not that I had time to worry about it. I still had to find Stephen. And I didn't have much time left.

I looked at the tickets in my hand. At least it turned out okay. He didn't hate me, and he knew I wasn't going to say yes. So he'd be better off finding a new lady to love him, I hoped—after all, he'd finally found the courage to let me know how he felt. But whether I would ask Tyler out? That was another matter. Fortunately, it was one I didn't need to worry about at the moment. I had a mission to accomplish.

Fourteen

I spent a second evening staking out the store at the student union and caught Stephen as he was picking up a big bag of barbecue potato chips and a liter of soda.

Happily, or not, he said yes. We were set to go out on Saturday night. Unless fate intervened and I found "the one" before then. Seriously, I think Mother Hubbard's writing about finding true love was the only way the campus was going to let her (me) out of this silly third-date challenge.

When I told Tyler he'd have to pay for two more tickets to the play, he just smiled and snagged two more from the paper's usual play reviewer. Cheapskate.

Turns out, she was happy to give them up because she hates Shakespeare and had planned to make up her review rather than sit through the play, so I didn't even have to feel guilty that we were using more free tickets.

I suppose I could be seen as taking Richie's suggestion that I use the tickets to ask Tyler out. After all, Tyler was coming to the play with me. Sure, he wasn't my date. And he was dating the girl he was crushing on big-time. I think Richie had meant me to ask him out separately, after the ouchy double date was history.

But I'm more like Tyler—a coward— than like Richie. The thought of asking Tyler out and hearing a no . . . there was no way I would take it as well as Richie had.

Besides, Tyler and I were going to the play together, sort of. So why did I waste more than a few minutes hoping that Richie wouldn't notice my foursome if he happened to glance out into the audience? I guess we cowards always think the brave will sneer instead of pity us for our lack of nerve.

Sophia was still unsuspecting of Tyler's

ulterior motive for asking her to come to the play with us. She was a girl who tended to focus on her own motivations. Which happened to be finding out if her wide dating pool was still a little too shallow.

It was kind of fun to be getting ready for our evening at the same time. And a little intimidating. Not that she didn't try to help me highlight my good points. "Use the plum on your eyelid. It'll bring out your eyes."

I examined the results in the mirror. "Isn't this too much drama?"

"Nope. Just the right amount of drama for a night of Shakespeare and romance."

"If I want to start something romantic with Stephen, I think I'll have to use silver eye shadow. Not to mention silver blush. Come to think of it, I'd be better off just going straight for the silver face paint. He doesn't make time for anything but his robots."

"Robots?" Her voice lifted and I remembered that Sophia liked to read science fiction for entertainment. To each her own, I guess. "That means he's smart."

"He probably has an IQ in outer space. But he doesn't talk, so who could tell."

"Smart guys are sometimes shy. Maybe he is just too overwhelmed by his feelings to show his heart to you."

I shrugged. "Maybe. I guess that's why he's getting another chance. But I think you and Tyler will agree with me by the end of the date. And maybe things can get back to normal for Mother Hubbard—and me. You know, back when I didn't have to go out with a guy I'd already written off?"

Sophia sighed. "It is so hard to know another person, isn't it? Do you think it is really like Professor Golding says? All chemicals and pheromones? No hearts at all?"

"I hope not. Because some people have great chemistry in the beginning, but they don't have anything going in the heart department." Like Blaine in charm mode.

"Yes. Chemistry is wonderful. But I believe in something more too. I just haven't found it yet."

"Let me know if you do."

She grinned. "Oh, don't worry, you'll know—if I find the one, I'm not waiting around to let someone else steal him."

"Not exactly a feminist statement, Sophia!"

"Of course it is," she replied smugly, adjusting her hair for maximum sexiness. "Women can have anything a man can— including someone to love and support them." She checked herself in the mirror, more worried than I thought she had any right to be. "Do you think Tyler and I would be good together?"

I pretended to be checking myself out, although I already knew I was as good as I was going to get. I didn't want to meet her eye when I answered that question. "I don't know."

She checked her teeth for lipstick. "I just don't see it. He is nice enough, and funny sometimes when he doesn't mean to be. So serious, though. I like a man who can laugh at himself."

"Isn't that the point of giving someone a chance? Just in case you're missing something? For all you know, Tyler can laugh at himself." I felt a little hypocritical, considering I'd just done this to Richie. But I consoled myself that that was different— I'd known Richie from kindergarten through high school. We'd studied together, sneaked each other chocolate during our SATs . . . if there'd been a spark there, I'd have known it.

"I suppose." Sophia adjusted my hair for the third time. What was wrong with it? "Personally, I think you and he are a better match."

That time I couldn't help looking at her. "So why did you say yes when he asked you out?"

"Because I like the idea of you going out with this last guy with a pair of chaperones, of course. Although I think you'd be better off taking more karate classes so you can make your *no* perfectly clear."

"I'm already registered for next semester." Sometimes I actually take the call the universe sends me. This one had been very clear: Not everyone is to be trusted.

Blaine probably wouldn't have pushed it, but no doubt there were guys who would have. One had even left comments on the blog to tell Mother Hubbard so. Something about the price of dinner. Professor Golding had blasted his Neanderthal attitudes in class for five minutes. She'd actually been shaking when she finished.

"Good. But I still think you should give it a try with Tyler."

Fortunately, the knock on the door and the arrival of the person in question stopped that conversation cold.

He came in, all eyes on Sophia, of course. "Ready to go pick up Space Cadet from his dorm?"

"First you must tell us how beautiful we look."

"You're gorgeous."

"Now Katelyn."

He looked at me. And took a second look. "Wow. You look even better than you did when you went out with Blaine."

"Thanks." I was sure that was supposed to be a compliment.

"Good thing we're going with you," he said, making himself a couple with Sophia with his words. "Or Space Cadet might try to morph into Hands-On Guy."

I thought of Stephen putting his arm around me. His hand on my knee. Nope. Not happening. I'd be lucky to get a peck on the cheek good night. So why did I agree to this again? Oh yeah, because I have a crush on the guy who is leading Sophia out the door. Her date.

Can you say weird? Then you have just a small idea of how I felt to be double-dating with Tyler, whom I had a crush on, to see a play featuring a guy who (I hope) just recently got over his crush on me. When you throw in that Tyler's date was the girl he was crushing on as well as my roommate—and she didn't view the evening as more than friends—and we're all going to see a university-level production of a lame Shakespeare comedy . . . Well. You have a really twisted sitcom episode.

Stephen had clearly taken his clothes out of the dryer sooner than usual. And he'd remembered to brush his hair (he had forgotten last time). So I was shocked when Sophia whispered, "Oh, he's a cutie."

I gave her an *are you kidding me?* look, but she just laughed and started talking about robots. Stephen lit up at finding someone to talk to. But you know what? Even though he was talking to Sophia, he was looking at me. Yeah, I guess I could see why she'd thought he was cute—with a little work he might even make it to semi-hottie. But the question was, did I want to be the girl to do that work?

Double-dating is interesting. You cut the work of conversation in half, but you add to the number of logistical decisions. We had a little awkward moment when we went to sit in the theater. Were we going to sit boy-girl-boy-girl, or were we going to sit boy-girl-girl-boy (no one even considered girl-boy-boy-girl)? Finally we decided that Sophia and I should be in the middle so we could whisper comments to each other and not annoy the guys.

When the house lights went down, signaling the beginning of the play, I couldn't help but feel relieved. No more conversation required. No more seeing Tyler looking at Sophia like he wanted to lick her from head to toe. Just a few more hours and a shared plate of nachos at the student union, and my third-date adventures would be over. For good.

Richie was Puck. Which was not as small a part as I'd remembered. I think he must have meant that his part was a small one as a joke because Puck was supposed to be a fairy and Richie was short enough to pull the role off.

But then, when Mr. Jamison made us read the play, I'd gotten so bored and confused that I'd resorted to a used CliffsNotes and a last-minute study session with my best friend, Claire—who loved Shakespeare and was now an English major at Penn State—to pass the unit exam.

At least tonight all I had to do was stay awake and remember to tell Richie that he was very good as the mischievous Puck. Through e-mail.

I think face-to-face would still be a little awkward. Maybe by next year we'd be able to share a glass of strawberry milk without feeling like we didn't know what to say. Maybe.

I had a chill down my spine when I realized what Richie had meant about the play being like my life. It was actually painful as I sat and watched all the characters longing for the wrong person and hurting the person who longed for them. Who knew that Shakespeare knew all about crushes gone wrong way back in the Dark Ages?

Don't know how I missed that part in high school. But then, I hadn't been open to the idea in tenth grade that David was the wrong guy. Or eleventh. Not until he asked me to the prom, actually. And by then high school was nearly over.

The play was a reflection of my life since I'd hit puberty. Lots of confusion and never knowing who was who. A little comedy, a little tragedy, and then a big bow at the end. The biggest difference I could see, besides the fact that I don't have to wear skirts that hit the ground, was that at the end of the play the women got roses, while at the end of college I would—I hoped—get a degree. Big whoop.

If human beings hadn't figured out a way around this crush thing in five hundred years, did that mean there was no cure except Shakespeare's magic? And maybe common sense. Although, come to think of it, Mother Hubbard's common-sense approach hadn't really helped me get over my crush on Tyler. By the end of the play I wanted the potion that Oberon, king of the fairies, finally sprinkled on the four lovers to rearrange them back into the right couples. Is that what it takes to cure the irrational attraction of crushes—a magic potion?

It had been sad to see the star-crossed lovers run amok, with Puck and the fairies playing them for fools.

Richie really knew what he was talking about—the characters were very much like us. Me. Tyler. Sophia. Stephen. Even Richie, though I think he may have finally escaped the curse of the unrequited crush. I hope. The only thing I couldn't figure out was whether Mother Hubbard was Puck, making things worse, or Oberon, who eventually straightens the whole mess out.

Fifteen

Okay. Maybe, just this once, the third time's the charm. Stephen turned out to be not only smart, but sexy in a shy wait-a-minute way. He also opened doors for me and made sure I got through before he followed me.

Maybe I was more relaxed because Tyler and Sophia had agreed to double-date and it didn't seem like such a lonely endeavor. Or maybe it was because the play had made me decide to take Mother Hubbard's advice—to forget about Tyler as anything but a friend, and really try to make a connection with Stephen. Common sense at its best.

I admit, I hadn't expected it to work so well. I'd figured I'd have to date a few more guys before I found one who could completely obliterate the crush I had on Tyler.

But what can I say? I noticed how Stephen paid attention to me and didn't forget I was his date, despite the fact that I was standing right beside Sophia. Which was neat. Then he asked me where I thought I'd be in ten years, and I looked past his wire-rimmed glasses into his eyes and . . . the buzz started, just like a switch had been flipped on inside me. Who'd have guessed?

Admittedly, Sophia had spent a lot of time drawing Stephen out, so even though I could see his good points, I wasn't the one encouraging him to explain where he thought the future of robotics would be in ten years over so-so Mexican food and drink (the student union has a food bar that manages a washed-out multiculturalism—blah Mexican, Chinese, and Greek kiosks, plus blah hamburgers and fries).

Four people out on a double date aren't absolutely safe, especially when two of the guys are really cute and one of the girls is hot. But we best-friend types know all about double-dating with hotties. We're not expected to carry the conversation. But it was nice, sitting there, watching Sophia crack Stephen's shy shell open like he was a nut and she was a nutcracker (which she has been called before, but in another context).

Stephen surprised me, though, as he happily answered Sophia's questions while we chowed down on nachos until there was just a smear of cheese left on the plate. Evidently he'd been reading Mother Hubbard's blog. Which was why he'd not only brushed his hair, but also picked out clean, unwrinkled clothes. After all, a clean guy gets more cuddle time, as the girls on the blog made clear.

Stephen was trying hard to get a clue. And the girls of the world had Mother Hubbbard to thank for that. And Mother Hubbard, via me, was very glad that someone was hearing what she was saying and making positive changes instead of snarky comments.

So, who was I to turn down a trip to Stephen's lab to see his robot?

"You will?" He seemed as surprised as he was pleased. He curved a smile that made the dimple in his chin stand out. Excellent.

"Sounds like fun." I love dimples almost as much as I love guys who don't take my affection for granted. The evening was bound to get better once it was just the two of us in a dimly lit lab, I could feel it down to my toes.

And then Tyler kicked me under the table.

"Excuse me." I shifted out of his reach and glared at him.

He was trying to send me some message with his eyes. What, I couldn't tell. "I thought you said you had a test Monday that you needed to study for tomorrow?" His eyebrows wiggled up and down like they'd come alive and were about to eat his face.

Oh. Memory jogged. In point of fact, I had not said that I had a test to study for. I had said that if the evening with Stephen was dragging on, I would use that excuse to end it. "I'm all studied out. I can take some time to see a robot."

"I, too, would like to see a robot." Sophia smiled at Stephen.

Who smiled back. "Great. We can all go." Why couldn't he make it clear he wanted to ditch them? To be fair, I couldn't figure out how to do it either, and they were my friends. I suppose I could chalk that up to yet another bad point about double-dating.

I tried the ladies' room maneuver with Sophia. But she didn't get my *let's talk* signal and just said she didn't have to go. Tyler looked as unhappy as I felt, but I knew he wasn't going to go home until Sophia did.

So, rather than the intimate, low-light lab "moment" for two, we had a high-light mega lecture moment for four. I have to admit, I hadn't appreciated how smart Stephen was until I saw his robot. It looked human. Really. Well, in a plastic sort of way. But still, better than the talking robots at Disney World. It moved smoothly and even replied independently depending on what Stephen asked, in a very limited way—although he planned much more as soon as he got the algorithm perfected. Whatever that meant.

For the first time I could understand why Stephen was so caught up in robotics. His project was cool. A life-size, lifelike robot that could answer questions.

Granted, at the moment she could only answer "I'm fine" to a question of "How are you?" and yes or no to whether she was cold (apparently she had a temperature sensor in her skin).

Even Tyler thought it was cool and asked a million questions. He said he'd written an article on the robot project his freshman year, when Jezzy was just a gleam in Professor Jernigan's eye and newly funded with a grant from the government.

I'd begun to think any alone time at all would have to wait for the next date. Date four! Wow, what a concept. There'd been so many times when I didn't think I'd ever get to date three, never mind want a fourth or fifth.

I guess thinking that there was a future to take care of little things like private time without a nosy friend and a sexy roommate was a good thing.

But I still wanted to get rid of said friend—and especially said roommate, who just happened to be an art major with a secret passion for robot design. Normally, I think that's cool. But not tonight when she could actually understand what Stephen was talking about enough to ask intelligent questions (mine had consisted of why they had made her eyes blue and her hair blond, and Stephen hadn't even known the answer to that because it had been someone else on the team who made those calls). Give me another year or two and I'd have enough real engineering courses to understand. But Sophia went straight for the aesthetics of creating a humanlike robot and she didn't seem to need any engineering classes to get what he was doing. Beauty and brains in one package. How could a girl get so lucky?

Of course, if I wanted to be selfish, I could just ask, how could a girl (me) get so unlucky?

Then I remembered something. When I'd been worried about this double date (I had been convinced that Stephen would be more boring than an evening of playing solitaire with fifty cards), Sophia had suggested that, just in case I was wrong, we should agree on a signal for her to take Tyler and leave Stephen and me alone.

That's what I get for being so sure of myself that I didn't even bother to remember the signal until it was almost too late. I was supposed to say, "Sophia, did you turn off the coffeemaker in our room?"

Which I did.

Sophia, who was examining the schematic of Stephen's robot, didn't even look up. "It has an auto timer, don't worry about it, Katelyn."

Great. Why even suggest a signal if you were going to ignore it? Of course, I could tell by the way she was hunched over the schematic that she had forgotten the signal just like I had. Next time the signal would have to be something she couldn't possibly overlook. No. Strike that. Next time there would be no double date. No Sophia in the lab talking robotese with my date, leaving her date to fume—at me, of course, because darling Sophia could do no wrong. Guys!

The only good thing was that Stephen was talking to Sophia, but he was clearly looking at me. Me. The best friend. The not-so-hottie. It felt amazingly great.

I tried, last-ditch effort, to talk Tyler into getting Sophia out of there. After all, he had asked her because he wanted to go out with her, not just to protect me. "Don't you want to walk Sophia home alone?"

"Well, yeah." Funny how Stephen's interest still couldn't quite erase my chagrin that Tyler had a crush on Sophia. "But it doesn't look like she's ready to leave. I think she's going to make him take Jezzy apart and put her back together again."

"Yeah. I didn't know there was anyone else besides Stephen so into robots."

He looked at me for a second, and I knew he'd heard the distinct lack of enthu siasm in my voice. "Why did you come to see the lab if you're not that into robots?"

"I think I'm into Stephen." I felt funny saying it out loud. But I thought if I did— to Tyler, especially—it would make my resolution to move on even firmer than it already was.

"You do?" He looked at Stephen with an unhappy frown. I recognized that look—he was trying to figure out why both Sophia and I were paying more atten- tion to Stephen than to him.

I felt annoyed that Tyler wasn't happy for me. Sure, he didn't know that I'd decided to get over my crush on him and move on to Stephen. But still. I'd expect him to be happy for me—or at least happy that his Mother Hubbard challenge had landed him a big win for his point of view. "Isn't that exactly what you wanted to happen? For me to find a guy I liked on the third date when I'd previously written him off by the second?"

"I guess. But I didn't think Sophia—" He broke off, and glanced over at the two robotophiles. He shrugged.

"I know. Sucks to have your date pay more attention to someone else." Boy, did I know. Story of my life. "I wish I could think of a reason for you two to go home and leave me alone with Stephen."

"Maybe it's better this way, considering what happened last time." He didn't sound all that happy about it, but it was nice that he remembered the reason we'd double-dated in the first place.

"That was Blaine. This is Stephen. He hasn't even tried to kiss me yet, never mind pin me up against a bench so I can't move."

Tyler looked at me again. Really looked at me. It was beginning to be a habit. I still felt the buzz, but I ignored it. He grinned in that best-friend conspirator way, when you've just confessed something he can tease you with forever. "He just hasn't had the chance."

I laughed too. "Not all guys are like Blaine. And I don't think Stephen is like that."

We looked at Sophia and Stephen, who had taken Jezzy's face off. Tyler sighed. "It's not going to happen tonight. For either of us, unless we come up with something brilliant."

"So think of something."

"Like what?"

"I don't know, you're the creative one; you came up with the Mother Hubbard challenge, after all."

In the end it was the smart one—Stephen—who thought of something. Just as we reached the dorm and stopped for that awkward game of will we kiss or not, he said, in front of everyone (talk about courage), "I had a great time tonight, Katelyn. Would you like to go to a movie next Saturday?"

Life. Sometimes it is *very* sweet.

Just so you know, we didn't kiss, but I swear he was just about to get up the nerve when Sophia grabbed my hand and pulled me into the dorm behind her, calling a very cheerful "Ciao!"

I broke away, but it was too late; the guys had turned around and started walking away. There was no graceful way to recover the kiss moment.

I took my annoyance out on Sophia. "Hey! Why'd you do that? He was going to kiss me. I know he was."

"Well, I didn't want to give Tyler any ideas."

"You didn't have a good time?" Okay. So why did that make me feel good when I'd already decided to move on from Tyler? Because I'm an emotional roller coaster. Just like everyone else on this campus.

Sixteen

So. Mother Hubbard is happy today. You were right and I was wrong. Sometimes it seems that one more chance is worth taking.

If you want details about Third Date #3, all I'm saying is . . . he's smart, he's sexy, and I'm keeping the rest top secret because I don't want anyone else giving him another chance. I want him all to myself.

So what does this mean for the column? It means that you've all won a kinder, more compassionate Mother Hubbard. So keep reading— and don't be afraid to bring me your dating woes. I promise to answer on gentle cycle instead of putting everyone through the wringer.

Mother Hubbard

I was so happy to be happy that I didn't even mind Professor Golding using Mother Hubbard's turnaround as a launch for class discussion.

"Did all of you read the Mother Hubbard column this morning?"

There was a pretty loud yes from the group, which surprised me. I knew the blog had been fairly busy, but I still didn't think, in raw numbers, that so many people were so interested in what Mother Hubbard was up to that they'd bother to read the column before 10 a.m. I guess the whole how-to-find-true-love question was something we were all interested in. We have to kiss a lot of frogs and all that, true. But kissing frogs, when you think about it, is no fun.

"It seems our Mother Hubbard has discovered that sometimes a third chance makes all the difference."

Our Mother Hubbard? When had I become *our* Mother Hubbard?

"And not only Mother Hubbard has benefited from giving someone a third date. I'm impressed at how many of you took advantage of my offer for extra credit. There were quite a few of you revisiting old flames last week."

I was impressed too. Because her class was so big, she had a teacher's assistant and a classroom assistant. They each had a stack of papers six inches thick that they slapped down on a table for people to come up and retrieve in the Pick-up Sticks style of paper return—something a class this big can't avoid because a roll call return of papers would take an entire class period.

As everyone rushed down to sort through the stacks, I stayed in my seat. I couldn't help but wonder if the dating-supported businesses on and around campus had taken a big spike upward in profits, as I looked at everyone who'd written a paper (and there would still be a big stack left on the table, because the class was only about three-quarters full).

Professor Golding continued lecturing

as soon as the first mad, noisy rush for papers had died down, not waiting for the people who couldn't find their papers right away to get back to their seats. "In fact, I'm so impressed that I want to take a moment to discuss what I've learned in reading your papers."

I had not done the extra credit. I just wasn't willing to risk it. It was starting to become obvious that if I were revealed to be Mother Hubbard, my life—at least on this campus—would be over. Even after the revelation that Mother Hubbard had taken a more compassionate turn.

Now that I'd decided to give an actual mutually admiring guy a shot at being "the one," I absolutely did not want to leave campus.

"The two most striking themes I'm discovering is that most of you are looking for 'the one.' Defined, for most of you, as the person who gets you and still makes you feel good about yourself. So 'getting to third date' may happen on the actual third date, the tenth, or for one of you, the first. You may be going through a lot of people looking for that 'getting to third date' moment when you know you've found something real—but you do plan to stop once you find it."

We laughed.

"The other thing I found is that everyone has, at one time or another, felt something for someone who didn't return the feeling. So you're not alone. In fact, one paper—whose writer got a well-deserved A, I might add—even went so far as to suggest that human beings pursue relationships with the same single-minded blindness to disaster that lemmings do."

There were no laughs at that one. Lemmings have the reputation for swimming to their deaths. Who wanted to be a lemming? Besides, I think half of us didn't believe the unnamed writer (the half in relationships) and the other half didn't want to (the half not in relationships).

I was having fun with Stephen. He'd told me how much he enjoyed taking a break now and then from his robot-related life. We'd gone to a chick flick together, and we'd even Rollerbladed along the campus trails. Neither one of us was very good, which meant we had a lot of fun, and ended up with a few bruises and a nice precrash kiss, too.

On the fourth date I found out he was a good kisser, and I'm pretty sure he found out the same thing about me, because he no longer hesitated before kissing me, and his arm was always wrapped around my shoulder or my waist when we were out—or in, for that matter.

I especially liked being able to stop by after my last class and check on Stephen, who was almost always in the lab working on the robot. As usual, I let myself in through the big metal lab door and made my way around the parts and widgets that the robotics lab always had lying around on every flat surface.

I found him bent over Jezzy, as usual. I had just a moment to feel a little bit jealous before Stephen saw me. Then his face lit up and he pushed his glasses up and came to give me a hug. I held up the bag with his dinner—a sandwich I'd picked up in the student union—but he took the time for a long kiss before he noticed.

"Food. How did I ever survive without

you?" He held up his hands apologetically. He was holding a screwdriver in one hand and a soldering iron in the other. I'd hung out with him long enough to know this was strange. He should have had solder instead of a screwdriver. Soldering irons are useless unless you have solder to go with them.

Then I noticed Sophia, crouching down behind the robot's back, frowning intently at the freakishly humanlike arm. She held the solder. Not long after our initial double date, Stephen and I had convinced her to join the robotics team since she was so into it.

Stephen turned to her. "Katelyn brought food."

Uh-oh. "I didn't know anyone else would be here, so I only brought one sandwich and a bag of chips."

"No problem, we'll share." He put down his tools and snatched the bag from me. "Did you already eat?"

"I'm going to hit the dining hall later, but I knew better than to expect you to join me."

"It's nice to have someone who gets

me," Stephen said as he popped open the bag of chips.

I knew just what he meant. "How's it going?"

He answered through a mouthful of chips. "Two steps backward and one step forward, I'm afraid."

"No wonder you're hungry."

He popped open the soda, and then stopped. He looked at the food he was stuffing in his face, surprised. "I guess so. I hadn't really thought about it."

No surprise there. "When did you eat last?"

"This morning?" He wasn't even sure. I loved that about him. So serious about his work he forgot to eat.

Sophia stood up and stretched. Even in jeans and a ratty sweatshirt—her robot work clothes—she looked good. "Do you like ham and cheese?" Stephen asked her.

She nodded as she came over and snatched some chips from the bag. "My favorite."

"I didn't realize you'd still be here. I thought you were going to check out that new club with Frodo or Fredo or whoever."

"Frederick. No, I canceled." She looked at Jezzy, who lay with the metal skeleton showing under a separation in the human-like skin covering. "If we're going to have a shot at winning this competition, we have to pay attention to the details. And that takes time."

"We're just trying to get this last application of falskin to ripple authentically over the forearm," Stephen added. "The competition is over Thanksgiving break, you know."

"I know," I replied.

Stephen had dragged an old uphol-stered armchair that the grad students were getting rid of into the lab as a place for me to sit and keep him company while he worked. We scrunched into the chair together while he finished eating his half of the sandwich. And then they were back to work again.

I half wanted Thanksgiving break to get here soon, and half didn't want it to come at all. I wouldn't see Stephen for a week because I'd be at home and he'd be at the competition. But, on the bright side, the competition would be over, Jezzy would have her blue ribbons or gold stars . . . or not . . . and I wouldn't have to fight a robot hussy for boyfriend time anymore.

I hung out with them, watching as they fussed over the robot—which looked pretty good to me.

Maybe I wasn't cut out to be an engineer, because I really thought they'd put enough time in. But it was a mistake to say so, I guess.

"Looks great to me. But what do I know?"

"You're going to be a mechanical engineer. You know," Sophia said.

"Right." I wasn't going to broadcast that I wasn't as into my major as they were into theirs. Passion was a good thing, in a relationship and in a major. But maybe I just needed to give it some time. That's what my dad said, anyway.

"I'm going to hit the dining hall." I stood up and walked over to look down at Jezzy's blank face. "Maybe I could come back after, and we could go check out that new comedy club the union is hosting tonight?"

Stephen and Sophia both looked at me with a blank look that was so much like Jezzy's, it gave me the creeps.

I sighed. "Never mind. I'll just join the Gossip Girls in the common room tonight."

Stephen kissed me good-bye with a worried little smile. "You do get how important this is, don't you?"

"Of course I do." I was trying, anyway. "Good luck."

I confess, I heard a little voice asking me whether Tyler might want to hang out with me. I felt a little guilty. But only a little. It's not like my crush on Tyler had ended instantly because I'd decided to move on. No one who could crush on a guy for four years in high school is that fickle. It had just receded—the buzz factor when we were together was much lower. Almost the sound of a refrigerator from a room away.

But, because I was spending a lot of time with Stephen in his lab and Sophia was too, Tyler had been avoiding us. Our quick meetings to exchange the column were so quick I almost had to pick whether to say hi or bye because I didn't have time for both. Either way, he was out of the picture, and Stephen and I were in it— together. Better to keep it that way. So I hung out with the Gossip Girls and pretended I didn't mind that my boyfriend preferred a robot to me. It was only temporary, after all.

Everything was going great until Stephen and I had our first fight. I'd stopped counting dates; they had started to blur to the point where we were just a couple. The fight began as just a little thing. I thought. It started with my asking if he thought working with robots was the most important thing in the world. Yeah. Not a smart question.

All I really wanted to hear was that I was more important than robots. Just by a smidge, not by loads.

Yes, yes, I know. If I'd asked Mother Hubbard's advice, even the new compassionate Mother Hubbard would have been blunt: too much too soon. What can I say? I was a little greedy. I knew it. But I couldn't stop myself.

So we had a mega fight over something

really stupid. Just like a thousand other couples. We all know the story. Some couples fight and stay together, and some fight and don't.

The problem was, since this was our first fight, I didn't know which we were going to be. I didn't even know which I wanted to be. I mean, how can anyone think robots are more important than girlfriends?

We'd gotten into the habit of eating dinner together every Friday night, Jezzy or not. In a different dining hall, just so we wouldn't attract a crowd that would distract us from each other. So when he canceled on dinner the first Friday after our fight, I didn't like it, but I wasn't going to drive myself crazy over it.

Okay. I did drive myself crazy over it. But in a controlled way. I complained to Sophia.

If I'd thought about it, I might have guessed she wouldn't be supportive. She'd been spending all her spare hours at the lab herself. "You know his robots are important to him."

This was not what I wanted to hear. So

I tried again. "You sound like you're defending him. Shouldn't a girlfriend be more important?"

She wasn't really in a sympathetic mood. "This is his career, his dream. Should a girlfriend want him to give up his dreams for her?"

"I get that he has dreams." Well, I wanted to. But robots? Okay. If he had to dream about robots, I guess I could be cool with that. "I just want to be first."

She hadn't been looking at me as we talked. But now she did. I was surprised at how passionate she was when she answered, "Then he is the wrong guy for you. His robots will always come first with him. What would Mother Hubbard say?"

I guess it took her being harsh for me to get it. "She'd say I was pushing, which is applying force in the wrong direction if I want to keep seeing him."

She nodded. "Right, she'd use that physics stuff to explain the emotions. Good old Mother Hubbard. Who happens to be right."

I sighed. "So the physics of attraction says I was being a bitch, then? And he should hate me and never talk to me again?"

"No." My question seemed to soften her a little. "You were just letting jealousy make you unreasonable. We all do that sometimes."

"So what should I do? He won't talk to me. Can you make him talk to me?" I'd never seen any guy ever refuse Sophia anything she asked for. Surely Stephen would agree to talk to me? Wouldn't he?

"I don't know. . . ." She was reluctant, which I could understand. Getting in the middle of a boyfriend-girlfriend fight could be dangerous to your health and your sanity.

"Look. I promise I'm not doing the 'poor me' thing. I just want to talk to him. We can work this out, or break up. Whichever." Not that I really believed we would break up—I do know how to hang on to the last shreds of hope, after all. "I just don't want to do the wimpo route of never speaking to each other again and letting things fade away."

She still didn't look too enthusiastic. "Okay. That's fair. I don't like that wimpo stuff either."

Ummm. Yeah. That was why I used the argument. "Thanks, Sophia."

"How about this? The competition is soon. On the flight home I'll have time to talk to him when he isn't so stressed."

"Not until the competition?" I didn't like that suggestion.

"It isn't that far away. We leave tomorrow and we'll be back after Thanksgiving break."

"Okay. Thanks. You won't regret it." It was better than nothing, especially since Stephen wasn't talking to me and he had to talk to Sophia.

"Let me talk to him first, then we'll see if I regret it." She had this semiguilty look. I couldn't figure out whether she thought things were over between us or not, but I didn't care. She was going to help me talk to Stephen. I knew that with a little communication, I could make him see that we could get past this. That I wouldn't be the kind of girlfriend who made him give up his dreams.

I hugged her. I couldn't help myself. "Really. Thanks."

"Just concentrate on having fun at

home. First time back home after college is always fun—you're trying to be adult and they're trying to get their little girl back."

Crap. I'd forgotten that little detail. I'd not only have to wait to hear from Sophia, I'd have to deal with my parents and my brother and all the questions they'd ask me about college life. My mother was sure to ask if I was seeing anyone. So what should I tell her?

"You promise you'll talk to him on the plane?"

"I promise."

"I'll keep my cell on, then. You've got my number, just in case he dumped it off his phone because he thought I was the worst bitch in the world."

"I'm sure he doesn't think you're a bitch, Katelyn." She smiled, and I could tell that her experience with guys was so much more than mine that she understood this whole thing better than I did. "I don't know if you want to do this on the phone, though. Maybe in person is better?"

"I just want this to be fixed as soon as possible." She wrote down my home number, even though she had my cell on her cell too. She was humoring me. But I was willing to be humored if it meant I could talk to Stephen a little sooner than Sunday night when we were all back in the dorm after Thanksgiving break.

Time at home after being in the dorm was . . . interesting. It did prove that college had changed me in ways that high school hadn't. Maybe just because I was living on my own and I'd learned to trust myself a little. I'd also learned to like not being on the parental watch list.

Unfortunately, my parents hadn't changed. They still wanted to know every place I went and when I would be home. And my mother got still every time I took out my cell phone and checked it to see if I'd missed a call. I hadn't. And believe me, I checked often enough to know.

Because she was worried about me, my mom took me shopping and to dinner before dropping me off at the dorm. Which meant I got back very late on Sunday. Sophia was nowhere to be found. Probably out at a hot club since she'd been club deprived while they were working on the robot competition. Sometimes it is inconvenient to have a hottie socialite for a roommate, even if she is willing to try to get your boyfriend to talk to you again.

Before I'd had a chance to hear whether or not Sophia had been successful with Stephen, Tyler knocked and came into the room without waiting for my answer.

He was smiling. One of those big *I've got great news* smiles that I hadn't seen on his face since Mother Hubbard had become a more compassionate and less controversial figure on campus.

"Guess what? WEDU called. They want to interview Mother Hubbard on her change of heart about third dates." WEDU was the campus radio station. I never listened to it because it either played whacked-out music from bands no one had ever heard of before, or featured whacked-out commentators rambling on about the environment, the—almost nonexistent—club scene, or the Goth subculture that I couldn't care less about.

The whole idea stank. And since I was stressed about not hearing from Sophia, I said so more bluntly than I might have otherwise. "Are you out of your mind? A radio interview? Why don't you just publish my name next to the column?"

He ignored my argument. "It's just a campus station. And the blog has been dead since Mother Hubbard turned good. We could use the boost."

I flipped open my cell phone. No message. "Duh. I'm anonymous, remember? I know not many people listen to the radio station, but some of them will probably recognize my voice."

My sarcasm had started to cut through his enthusiasm. "Duh. They've agreed you can have your voice disguised, so that it won't be recognizable?" He gave me a pleading puppy dog look, his head cocked in a way that had always made me say yes before. "Don't you think I'd look after you?"

"Sure you would." Right after he looked after the bottom line. What is it about having something to prove that made us all just a little insensitive?

But then he said, "Don't worry, I'll be there to hold your hand."

"You will?"

"I've got it all arranged. We'll use my cell phone. We can do it right here."

"How will I disguise my voice? Or will the station do it?"

"I didn't want to take that chance. They can be flaky there." Tell me about it. They'd once played ten minutes of someone snoring to prove to him that he snored. Not that I heard the show, just everyone talking about it afterward.

"I got this." He held up a voice distorter. Funny, I'd watched a lot of TV crime shows and movies, but I'd never really noticed what they did to distort voices. It was a weird little box thing that I just had to hold to my throat, and voilà, I sounded like an octogenarian who'd been smoking from the time I could light a match.

Goody. I was going to be on the radio. I wondered if Stephen would hear me? But mostly I wondered why he hadn't called.

"When is this interview?"

"Tonight."

"Are you kidding me?"

"Hey. They have a hole to fill. We have

to take our opportunities where we can get them."

"Fine." It wasn't like I had anything better to do. Until Stephen called or Sophia came home.

Seventeen

Tyler showed me the list of questions the radio host had e-mailed him. Not too many. Not even bad questions. Maybe a little boring, but I could handle boring.

Using a voice-distorting box to answer questions this bland made me feel like I should be confessing to a crime. I mean, really, who wanted to know if Mother Hubbard preferred boxers or briefs?

Even my boyfriend—should it happen that Stephen did call, did talk to me, did make up with me—shouldn't have to take my opinion on that subject into account. I certainly wasn't going to wear thong underwear on his say-so.

I thought about how to answer one question about whether I was still happy that I'd gone out on the third date. Tricky, since technically I hadn't spoken to Stephen since our big fight. I *wanted* to be happy again, but I was at least a day away from making it happen. Not that I was going to confess that on the radio—even using a voice distorter.

"What if some of my nosy dorm-mates overhear the weird sounds of the voice distorter?"

In typical Tyler fashion, he waved away my concerns.

Apparently, however, he wasn't as unaware of the possibilities of discovery as I'd feared. Because, when Sarah Miller from next door knocked on the door and said, "Why is this door locked? Are you dying in there?" he turned off the lights, dragged me to the door, opened it, and kissed me full on the lips.

Then he looked at a gaping Sarah and said, "Does something look wrong?"

Sarah, the gossip of the dorm, looked carefully at me.

I confess I wasn't much help. I just

looked at her with a muddled expression. Tyler had kissed me. In very short order it was going to become clear to everyone Sarah met that Tyler had kissed me.

It was a good thing she couldn't hear the buzzing in my head that had started even before he kissed me. Had started as soon as I realized what he was going to do. Had started despite the fact that I still wanted Stephen to call. Was I ever going to get over my crush on Tyler?

This might even be worse than my being exposed as the voice behind Mother Hubbard. Might be worse than never giving a third date. He'd crossed the line between friend and boyfriend without warning.

And he kissed better than Stephen.

Sarah smiled, happy to have a tidbit of gossip. "I knew it." Then she bounced off down the hall to spread the news.

Sophia said Sarah just needed to get a man. But I think Sarah would devour any man who came near enough. She was just the hungry type—hungry for gossip, guys, and good grades. A part of me could relate. The rest of me didn't.

"Why did you do that? She's going to tell everyone that she caught us making out."

"Is she—or anyone else in the dorm—going to wonder what we're doing when the interview starts?"

"No, but . . ." I would have pointed out the obvious flaw in his plan—people would now think we were a couple. But just then the phone rang. Not Tyler's cell phone. Mine.

We both looked surprised, and I think he was thinking the same thing I was. Someone had found out.

But no, I checked the number. "It's Sophia."

"Tell her to call back."

I had no intention of telling her to call back. I flipped open my phone and quickly said, "Sophia, I can't explain, but I have to do a radio interview in a minute, so just tell me right now if you got Stephen to agree to talk to me, and then I'll call you back after the interview to talk more."

There was silence on the other end of the phone, and for a minute I thought the call had been dropped. I saw Tyler looking at me in surprise, and I realized that he hadn't known that Stephen and I were not speaking. Great. One secret out. Let's hope we didn't make it two before the night was over.

"You have to do an interview? I will call back—"

"No way. I'm dying to know what Stephen said. I don't want to wait for you to come back."

Another silence. Then, "I'm not coming back."

"What? Where are you?"

"Seattle."

"What are you doing in Seattle? Did you get bumped from your flight?" I knew it had to be something big. I knew it. But still, I couldn't stop myself from asking, "So you haven't talked to Stephen yet because you haven't flown home yet?"

"I talked to Stephen."

Her voice didn't sound like Stephen had been willing to talk to me. I felt half guilty for not asking about Seattle, but I had waited five days to find out whether Stephen would talk to me. "What did he say?"

There was silence again. And then I heard someone say, "Do you want me to tell her?"

I couldn't help it—I sucked in air like I'd just been sucker punched. Stephen. And why was she letting him listen in on this conversation?

"Sophia. This is not funny. Where are you, and what are you doing?"

Sophia said, "Katelyn."

And then I knew. I just knew as if I'd always known. But sometimes even when you know something, you just don't want to believe it. "You're with Stephen now. My Stephen."

"We won the competition." All of a sudden, Sophia, who couldn't say anything much, started talking a mile a minute. "Jezzy was the best robot among two hundred other competitiors. Robodyne corporation offered us jobs. Real jobs. And we can finish our education here while we're working."

Jezzy won. Big whoop. I heard the way she said *we*. And I didn't have a good feeling in the pit of my stomach. You know how you can see the train coming. Hear it.

Feel the ground shaking. But still you wait a second. That's the way I felt when I asked, "*We* can finish *our* education?"

"I hope you understand. We didn't mean it. But we—we're just right. He makes me laugh, he challenges me, he—"

The train was coming, the ground was shaking, but still. "Right? For you? Are you telling me my boyfriend was right for you? I—"

Sophia said very softly, but clearly, "Even if I wasn't in the picture, he'd still be in Seattle working and going to school. Besides, you two haven't been happy together in a while, and—well, I'm sorry."

It doesn't matter if you see the train coming. It still hurts when it hits. "Sorry? That you stole my boyfriend? That you're going to change schools and live in Seattle?" I stared at the cell phone. Yep. It was Sophia's number. "Is this a joke?" I knew it wasn't, yet I still hoped she'd burst out laughing and tell me she was outside the door with Stephen waiting to forgive and forget.

"No. I hope you will forgive me one day."

"Forgive?" I didn't feel like forgiving her. At least, I didn't think I did, but at the moment I was too numb to tell for sure.

"Tell Tyler—"

"I know what to tell Tyler!" I was sharper with her than I'd meant to be. Because Tyler looked as shocked as I felt. He was staring at me. Following the conversation. From the look on his face, he didn't want to follow it any further than I did. Too bad for us.

My hand holding the phone began to shake as there was once again silence. Tyler sat down beside me and put his hand over mine. We both listened as Sophia said cautiously, "So, good luck on your exams."

"Just like that?"

"Have you ever known me to wait for something I know I want?"

It was my turn for silence. What was there to say to that? I hadn't known her very long, but I had lived with her. And no. I knew if I had lived with her for a million years, she would never have hesitated to go after something she wanted.

"You are a sweet girl, Katelyn. When are you going to give Tyler a chance? For all you know, he's the one for you."

Tyler stiffened and pulled away a little, just as Sophia said, for the last time, "Ciao!"

I knew this silence really meant it was over. I flipped my phone closed and resisted throwing it across the room. It wasn't the phone's fault Sophia had used it to rip my heart out long-distance.

Give Tyler a chance, she said. Right. How does she expect me to give a guy a chance who only looks at me from time to time? But I forgave her. She was in love. And love, as they say, is blind.

I couldn't help myself—I started to shake, as if I'd been out in a snowstorm in a T-shirt and shorts. I didn't want to cry. Especially in front of Tyler. But I couldn't help it. The tears just came. And they wouldn't stop. Even though he put his arms around me and held me so tight I could barely breathe.

I think we might have sat there all night that way. If Tyler's cell phone hadn't rung.

He reached for it quickly, and I knew, I just knew he was going to tell the interviewer to forget it. I took the phone from him and turned on the voice distorter. It was interview time. And Mother Hubbard's voice was so choked up, she almost didn't need help to disguise it. But she had something to say, and she was going to say it.

His name was Ralph the Mouth. And I could tell he was prepared to sneer at the whole concept of love, relationships, and advice on finding "the one." "So, Mother Hubbard. Rumor has it you're over a century old."

I answered the way Tyler and I had agreed I would, as if I were speaking from a long-ago era. "My tradition is, yes. But there are many who have carried on that tradition through the years."

"But not with such controversy."

"The current contretemps is merely a tempest in a teapot. It will blow over as soon as finals week comes along." I hoped I sounded like somebody channeling a hundred-year-old spirit. I certainly felt that old—shock can do that to a person, I hear.

I had the list of questions Ralph was

going to ask. Tyler had gone over them with me. We'd decided on a simple is better approach, and no ad-libbing allowed. I had intended to answer like Mother Hubbard—and to remember, as Tyler said, to keep plugging the paper as a must-read for anyone listening.

Not that anyone listened to the campus station, anyway. Or so I thought, when I decided to throw away the script and ad-lib right from the heart. I did spare one moment worrying whether Tyler would forgive me for it.

Of course, I stopped worrying about that when the interviewer dropped the normal line of questioning.

I quickly realized the questions the guy had e-mailed me were meant to soften me up. Leave me unprepared for the harder questions he meant to ask. Like the left turn he took after our previously fairly polite exchange.

"So, Mother Hubbard, do you think you might be a lesbian?"

"No!" The voice distorter made the word a loud and horrible croak.

Unapologetic, Ralph the Mouth

plowed on. "You're not homophobic, are you?"

"No." Poor Ralph. He had picked on the wrong person at the wrong time if he thought he was going to put words in my mouth. "I may be done with men, though. But not because I find women attractive— just because all men are rats and aren't worth all the trouble they cause." The distorter made my words harsher than I meant them. Or maybe not.

"Whoa. Mother Hubbard. I thought you now believed in the power of granting a poor guy a third date. Don't tell me you've changed your mind? I'd be so sorry to hear that." Right. Ralph's voice was smarmy with delight.

I didn't even bother with the antiquated language. I told it like it was. "Of course you're sorry. You're a guy, aren't you? Just like the guy who was such a coward he couldn't tell me it was over between us—just ran away to another university." And another woman—but I didn't think I could say that last part aloud without breaking down, no matter how angry I was.

"So which date was it that went bad?

Fifth? Sixth? What's the new rule for Mother Hubbard and her readers?"

"Just be friends. That's the new rule. Forget dating. Just be friends."

Even Ralph was startled into silence by that one. But then, laughing, he said, "Do you think anyone will take you seriously? I mean, come on. Sex, love, hooking up, dating, whatever you call it, that's what makes the world go round. Or at least the songs say so."

"Well, maybe it's time to make the world stop going round. At least then we won't get dizzy and sick, lose our balance, and fall down."

"You heard it here first, folks. Mother Hubbard is on the vengeance wagon. I bet this campus hasn't seen anything yet like a hundred-year-old woman scorned. Let's hear that one again, folks, shall we?"

He'd cut me off mic so I couldn't say anything else. Not that I wanted to. I'd said plenty already. More than plenty, I realized.

"I'm going to regret that in the morning, aren't I?"

I looked at Tyler, and he looked at me

and shrugged. "I think we both will. But what can you do? Did Sophia really transfer schools?"

My hero. Riding to my rescue. Not.

Eighteen

Well. You were right. No one will ever say Mother Hubbard can't admit when she was wrong. Mr. Smart and Sexy was a great third date. And fourth date.

He was a lousy breaker-upper, though. Just when I thought we had a chance. So sometimes the third date can be worthwhile. I got a great broken heart from this experiment. Thanks. A lot.

But, more important, I get the message: Don't tell you the truth. Sugarcoat the dating facts. So from now on Mother Hubbard's advice

will have two parts: the sweet lie and the bitter truth. Read whichever one you want to believe.
Mother Hubbard

Ralph had a great time playing the radio interview over and over again. Tyler didn't want to print my column. But I told him I'd never speak to him again if he didn't. I think, after the Sophia thing, he just wasn't quite ready for that one. So he printed it. And the campus went wild. If I thought they'd talked about me too much before . . . I started carrying my iPod everywhere to tune out the world around me.

But even the earbuds couldn't keep me from assimilating the campus opinions. A bitter fall—everyone said it was great that Mother Hubbard got past the third date, but they seemed even happier when she got dumped. And, for some reason, the stupid adage about getting back on the horse was everywhere—on the blog, in the letters to the editor, and even on a banner outside the student union.

Apparently the consensus was that Mother Hubbard would get over it. It wasn't a consensus I agreed with. In fact, little old me had retreated to bed two days into the whole thing. I'd tried to be strong. But then Professor Golding started another Mother Hubbard discussion and I lost it. I left class before I could hear what she—and the rest of the class— had to say about this latest twist in the Mother Hubbard history. And I decided to do a Rip van Winkle and sleep until it was all over and done with. After stocking our—oops, I mean *my*, because Sophia was gone—tiny dorm fridge with Ben & Jerry's ice cream—Karmal Sutra, of course.

The bad thing was that I was running out. There was a little Chunky Monkey, but that wasn't going to cut it. I was in heavy-duty broken-heart recovery. Still in ICU stage. And Sookie had flat-out refused to go get me some more when I called to beg her to help.

I thought she was the meanest person ever, until there was a knock on the door and Tyler appeared, with more Karmal Sutra and a worried frown.

"Midterms are coming up, kid. The

doctor's got a double dose of meds to get you up and out of that bed."

Tyler didn't give Sophia's empty side of the room—I'd packed her stuff up and taken it to the RA's room so she could mail it to Sophia in Seattle—a second look. His concern was all for me. Which, I have to admit, helped even more than Rocky Road for soothing a broken heart.

With the added danger of breaking it again before it was even healed, of course.

"I don't want to get out of bed. I just want to lie here and eat ice cream and never go anywhere again." Which was true, if completely self-indulgent and practically impossible to do.

"That's not the Mother Hubbard I know."

"It's the new Mother Hubbard. Wait until you see my next column." Which I hadn't written, except in my head. Annoyingly, the question was what to do when your roommate runs away with your boyfriend. And Mother Hubbard's answer was always the same—concentrate on my classes. Be the best engineering student I could be. Count myself lucky to be rid of Stephen. And Sophia, too.

So why didn't my heart respond with a quick healing—and my midterms benefit from extra study? Because, gosh darn it. I am a human being, and human hearts are not susceptible to common sense. Especially not broken human hearts.

"Do you have a column for me?" Tyler sounded so hopeful, I felt guilty I couldn't hand in a column in exchange for the ice cream.

"Not yet. Can you do it?"

"Okay." He sounded like he had something to tell me that he wasn't sure I wanted to hear.

I dug the spoon in again and said, "Spill it, Tyler. What else do you have for me besides ice cream?"

He tried not to grin. He really did. Which was some comfort. Not. "The radio interview got picked up by the *News and Courier*."

"Are you kidding?" I asked, but I really didn't believe he meant it. I thought he was trying some kind of wacko shock therapy.

He held up a copy. The headline read BROKEN HEARTS ON CAMPUS: SHOULD STUDENTS BE LOOKING FOR "THE ONE" OR THE 4.0?

Why was it especially galling to find that the campus—and the local newspaper—was even more interested in a brokenhearted Mother Hubbard? I don't know. But it was.

I guess the writer was long out of college, because the article came down firmly on the side of libraries and books. And the old Mother Hubbard. The one, the reporter said, with attitude.

"The local TV news wants you to do an interview with them." I could tell he thought I should do it. But he wasn't going to come out and say so, because, after all, I was a girl in my pj's at four in the afternoon—eating ice cream and wearing ear buds that weren't currently attached to an iPod.

An interview with the local news. Were they kidding? No. They weren't. It was a sign. A sign that it was time to return to my sensible alter ego.

I, Katelyn, was about to give Mother Hubbard a run for her money.

"Forget it, Tyler. I'm not going to do the interview, or the column, anymore."

You'd think I'd told him I was going to cut off his arm. "Katelyn, I'm counting on you."

"Well, stop, or you'll get your heart broken, just like I did. Or haven't you heard? Mother Hubbard is a bitter old cow who doesn't know how to handle disappointment."

He sat down on the bed next to me. This required more bravery than you might imagine since I hadn't showered or brushed my hair in days. With one finger he dug into the ice cream container I was cradling and scooped out some ice cream for himself. "Don't let them win, Katelyn. Show them Mother Hubbard is not bitter, old, or a cow."

He said a lot more, but mostly he just sat there and ate ice cream and listened to me complain about how unfair life was. He flinched a little when I said Sophia's name, and we had to get a new carton of ice cream when I came to the subject of Stephen. I don't know how he did it. But just by sitting there and eating ice cream with me in the dark, he did convince me to do the darned interview.

"On one condition." I couldn't believe I was caving in again. To Tyler. But I was. "I'm not going to the station. They'll have to interview the blogging Mother Hubbard. You can be the talking head. You're good at it."

He got that wheedler look in his eye. "What about—"

But I'd given as much as I was going to. "No more voice distorters. No brown paper bags over my head. Or no interview."

"Done." He took another scoop of ice cream with his finger. And then he hugged me. Hard. "Welcome back, Mother Hubbard."

I pushed him away, despite the definite buzz that was demanding I pull him closer. "That's another condition. I quit the column as soon as this is over."

I prepared for the interview by pretending I was talking directly to Sophia and Stephen. Traitors to me, but not to their own feelings. I must have had enough ice cream to make me see the light. Or make me light-headed. They loved working on robots together. They belonged together. So why couldn't I make it hurt less?

Tyler was right. If I was going to stay on campus and not run away, I needed, for my own sake, to make up for the unfortunate radio interview. I would never have done that interview in technipain ad-lib if I'd had time to think about it.

I didn't really want to leave Mother Hubbard on that bitter note. It wouldn't be fair to the person who took up the column when I quit. And someone would take it up, because it was a century-old tradition. Just because I didn't believe in Mother Hubbard didn't mean the tradition wouldn't continue.

So come interview time, I sat on the bed with my laptop on my lap and IM'd with the TV anchorwoman. It was quiet and dark in my room, and I felt a million miles away and completely disconnected, even though I knew that there were probably thousands of viewers who would see me IMing.

The questions were predictable, and light as cotton candy.

>Do you regret making your dating life public?

No. It's not like everyone else doesn't have a breakup story to match mine. And it helps to know that. A little.

>Still, to be so public with your personal pain must be hard.

No one knows who I am.

>True. And there's been some call for Mother Hubbard to come out of her cupboard. Will you ever reveal your identity?

I haven't in the last hundred years. And I'm going to keep it that way. Mother Hubbard isn't one person. She's a hundred-year-old everywoman.

There was a time delay so they could cut the interview in with something that would be more visually interesting, so when I logged off from the interview after the inevitable quick reporter kiss off/thank you, I turned on the TV to see them just introducing Tyler.

It made for funny TV, but those news guys know how to handle even interviewing through IM. Tyler was great—he reacted to the little rolling IM of my answers as if I were sitting there talking to him big as life.

The station even had an interview clip with Professor Golding, whose sound bite was "The college years are meant for exploration. Sure, there can be some heartbreak, but generally everyone learns to navigate relationships just a little bit better by the time they graduate. Mother Hubbard has helped students recognize that there are many ways to do this, but they're all difficult."

The only thing I wasn't sure I liked was the little graphic they'd whipped up, of Mother Hubbard sitting on her cupboard shaking her finger at the world. Her nose was way too long. She almost looked like a witch. *Maybe I should send them a new drawing of Mother Hubbard?* Nah, I flunked drawing in kindergarten—I was too stubborn to color things appropriately. I liked my suns blue and my grass pink. Or sometimes purple, if I was feeling pinked out.

But with this whole Mother Hubbard thing, I felt like the crayons available to me had been reduced to one. Brown. Mud brown. Mother Hubbard brown.

The reaction to Mother Hubbard's new return to third-date hesitation—and radio ranting—was overwhelming. Apparently, people were more enamored of Mother Hubbard's advice pre–getting to third date. So was I, for that matter. For different reasons. I believe in common sense and fewer broken hearts. The world at large just liked controversy. The messier, the better.

Things might have ended there. But they didn't. Who knew there really was such a thing as a slow news day? Not me. Until Tyler caught me just before I went into Human Sexuality class and pulled me away so no one would overhear him when he said, "We're going big time, what do you think of that?"

"Big time? Are you kidding?" I knew him well enough to know he wasn't. But I still hoped he would say he'd just decided to try to see how close I'd come to killing him. He didn't.

"You know that hot new MTV show, *Pimp My News*? They want us." He was practically floating a foot off the ground as he told me.

I guess I was still a little raw, because the look in his eye reminded me of the way Stephen looked every time he made some radical improvement in Jezzy. I stepped back. "*Pimp My News* wants to interview Mother Hubbard?"

Well. I guess when I wish for things to be different in college, I should be more specific. For example: me, no longer every guy's platonic best friend: good. But me, interviewing with the hottest new news show aimed at the eighteen to twenty-four crowd: not so good.

Nineteen

"We can't possibly do *Pimp My News*." I couldn't help being shrill. My life was going crazy—in a bad way. I wanted to be done with Mother Hubbard. And MTV thought the Mother Hubbard broken-heart story was worth an interview? Were they crazy? "What could they possibly see in us? And I do mean see, by the way. Or have you decided that you don't mind being the editor who lets out the secret of Mother Hubbard's identity?"

"That's the beautiful part. When I told them that Mother Hubbard had a century-old tradition of anonymity, they said they'd take any girl on campus who had followed

Mother Hubbard's advice. I picked you. Because we're friends. And you had that thing with Stephen and that thing with Richie, too." I stuck a mental Post-it note up to remind me never to tell Tyler anything ever again. He'd seen the Stephen thing. But I hadn't had to blab about Richie.

Great. I'd caused my own trouble. Well, all I could say was that's nothing new. "So they want us to fly to New York? And be on TV? To discuss Mother Hubbard, who can't be there because she doesn't exist." My head hurt. "What would they expect me to even say? Broken hearts suck? Doesn't everyone already know that? Especially people our age."

Tyler stopped smiling for a minute, and I remembered that his heart had been through the shredder not that long ago too.

"I'm sorry." I stood up and paced. "I didn't mean that."

"Yes, you did." Tyler wasn't grinning, and he wasn't trying to hard sell me either. He was struggling to make sense of everything as much as I was. "Broken hearts suck. But it's what you do about it that matters. To everyone. Even the national news."

"Well, they don't need me, then. You can spread the news. You deserve this trip. You're the one who thought up the third-date challenge. You're the one who thought up the blog. You go. Leave me here."

"No." Tyler shook his head. "You're representative of all the women you've given advice to—I mean that Mother Hubbard has given advice to. You're not supposed to be Mother Hubbard. You're just the girl who tried her advice and got burned and then decided to try again, even though you've found dating in college to be a whole new animal."

"Have I now? Says who?"

"Says you. You say I don't listen, but I do—doesn't this prove it?" His voice got higher, and he did a bad imitation of me. "Forget the loser and get back out there and find someone who will treat you well."

"It proves you don't know me at all, Tyler. All it will take is one question from the *Pimp My News* guy about whether or not I am Mother Hubbard—and I'll spill the beans. I'm not a good liar. Not at all. Or haven't you noticed?"

"You can do it—especially when you know what it would mean if you actually told people who you are. You don't need any hate mail addressed directly to you, do you?"

"Why am I even talking to you? As soon as they come to their senses, they'll rescind the invitation."

"They might." He nodded. "The person who called was pretty up front about it. If big entertainment news happens, we'll get bumped."

"Then why don't we just bump ourselves first, before suffering that kind of humiliation?" I tried to work the humiliation card—it had become obvious to me over the past few months that Tyler didn't love being publicly humiliated.

"How could you possibly turn down a visit to *Pimp My News*? Do you know how many people they don't ask? It's an honor!"

"Well, so's dying for your country, but that's not something everyone signs up for, now is it?"

"Fine. You don't need honor. Don't

need glory. Don't even need fame. But consider this: It's a free trip to New York. All expenses paid. A night in a nice hotel. And you get a chance to have your say in front of more people than you'll ever see again in your lifetime."

I put my hands over my ears. "Stop."

He waited me out, which was surprising. I would never have tagged Tyler as the patient type. Of course, I'd never have tagged Sophia as the type to run off with her roommate's not-yet-officially-broken-up boyfriend either.

When I'd finally taken my hands from my ears and opened my eyes, he just said three little words that made me cave.

No. Not those three little words. I wish.

What he said was, "I need you to do this with me." *I need you.* Powerful words from a guy with a buzz factor of ten who brought me ice cream to heal my broken heart—a broken heart caused by another guy.

So, yes. Apparently I could be bought. The going price at the moment was starkly obvious and highly depressing. And it wasn't a free trip to New York, or a chance for twenty-five seconds of fame on MTV. No. It was a weekend in the Big Apple with Tyler.

It was a chance to be as brave as Richie had been. To make my move on Tyler. If nothing happened between us then, I might as well tie it up with a pretty pink ribbon and toss it in the Dumpster. The boy was not going to see me as anything but a best friend.

I hit the gym the morning we flew out, determined to be in the best shape I could. I had a black dress my mom had made me buy when I graduated from high school. She said every girl needed a little black dress she could throw on for special occasions.

If this wasn't a special occasion, I couldn't imagine what was.

So in went the black dress, my cutest pajamas—just in case—and my best dancing heels. New York clubs had to let in the two hot young things who were interviewed on *Pimp My News*, didn't they?

I hadn't ever stayed in a hotel room by myself. The flight the show had put us on—coach, not first class, but I'm not complaining—was okay. And at least I had Tyler sitting next to me—no weakness allowed when he was looking on. I'd had one breakdown in front of him and I needed to make up ground if I really wanted to try to make something happen between us.

We did our best not to be gawky tourist types. I'm not sure we succeeded, because the desk clerk and the bellman both had big smiles on their faces when we asked for rooms next to each other on the highest floor they could give us.

I felt like a princess for a minute. The show had sent us a fruit basket and a welcome note—to each of us, in our rooms. Very nice rooms too. Since my mom and dad liked Motel 6 when we traveled, all four of us crowded together, I was a little overwhelmed at the idea of a big, luxurious room all to myself. In the end it was the all to myself that got to me. Yes, it was a nice hotel room. But still, people were walking down the hallway and the heating unit was noisy. I'd had a hard enough time sleeping in my dorm room alone since Sophia left.

This was a thousand times more nerve-wracking.

I gave up around midnight and called Tyler's room (I would have just knocked on his door because he had the room on my left, but I kept thinking about how the hotel advised that you look through the peephole before you open the door). "I can't sleep."

"Want to try to get into a club?"

"We have to be up early tomorrow."

"So?"

"Okay."

He was knocking on my door so fast I wasn't sure he hadn't been ready to come if I called. I liked that thought— but I knew better than to trust it.

We headed out to do the club scene. We were all the way to the lobby when we realized we didn't have a clue where to look.

"Should we just walk a few blocks and see where people are lined up?" I didn't know which way to walk, but I also didn't know what else to suggest.

"Probably a great way to get mugged." Tyler looked uncertain. "I guess that would make a good editorial—how to survive getting mugged in New York City. Not that I really want to be the one to write it."

"I'm not writing it either. Maybe you can tell Sookie what happened—if we get mugged—and she can write it."

"Maybe."

We stood there for a minute. I think we might have chickened out if it weren't for the light over the concierge desk. I guess New York is not only the city that never sleeps, it's also got concierges who never sleep.

Or maybe we just had a really nice hotel. The concierge on duty didn't seem to think it was at all strange that we would be looking for something to do at midnight.

He gave us directions to three different clubs no more than four blocks away. And he made Tyler go back up to his room and change into something more appropriate. Apparently, Sophia's influence had rubbed off on me enough that I was dressed well enough. I suppose I had something to thank her for. Not that I would.

We didn't get into the clubs. Not old enough. I think Tyler took it harder than I did, because after the third club's bouncer just shook his head and pointed us away, he stuck his hands in his pockets and looked uncharacteristically uncertain.

"Sorry. I bet they'd let you in if you weren't with me. You look hot."

That wasn't hard to hear. But he clearly needed some cheering up. So I took his arm and draped it over my shoulder so that we stood together, staring at the gaudy wonder that was Times Square. "I don't care about the clubs. Have you ever seen anything like this before?"

"On TV. On New Year's Eve."

"Tyler. We're here. We're really here. Let's enjoy it."

"If they won't let us in . . ."

"Let's go to Serendipity for ice cream. Like in that movie." My stomach clenched, still a little upset after all the ice cream I'd eaten to get over Stephen. "Or maybe hot chocolate."

"Is that in Times Square?"

"Does it matter? I can't sleep anyway."

He shrugged but didn't take his arm off my shoulder. "Guess not, then."

We walked all over Times Square,

going wherever they'd let us in. We didn't get hot chocolate, but we did get to see an ad for *Pimp My News* that had our college ID pictures plastered a hundred feet high (okay, so that's an exaggeration, but you try looking at a bad head shot that's blazing on a video billboard in Times Square, and you'll lose your sense of proportion too).

I took a picture of the ad with Tyler in the foreground, just to document the fact that I'd—at least once—gotten to make my mark in Times Square.

Who knows what my life will be like once I get back. I mean, I have finals to take. And a new roommate to find.

MTV arranged for a taxi for us. So one more thing to add to my list of things I've done. I've ridden in a taxi in NYC. And it was everything the movies promised it would be. Fast, furious, and boy was I glad to get to the curb on Forty-third and Broadway.

Pimp My News was the hottest new show on MTV. It had the quirky offbeat news style of Comedy Central's *The Daily Show*, but had a take on the news more suited for a teen crowd. MTV billed it as news that was terminally hip. I guess that meant, for at least fifteen minutes, Tyler and I qualified as the same.

The receptionist was nice and didn't treat us as if we were just college students at all. "Welcome to MTV, Katelyn and Tyler. Please have a seat and Jessica will be right with you."

"I can't believe I'm really here," Tyler said in a low voice when the receptionist turned away to call Jessica, whoever she was, to come get us.

"I know." I'd always known Tyler cared about the journalism business. But here, it was like he was in heaven. He was taking in every detail, checking out every person who walked in and out of the doors, darting down one of two hallways.

He sat on the reception couch, but I could tell he'd rather be moving down one of the hallways himself. "I wonder which one we'll go through?"

"I'm sure Jessica will let us know." It took a little while for Jessica to show up, but we didn't mind, because we had fun watching the people. Some of them were famous, but we did well, not gawking like tourists.

When Jessica, who turned out to be an intern, came to get us and lead us to the greenroom, she asked if we'd like a tour.

Tyler said, "That would be excellent."

And it was. The room where they ran the show was fascinating. Noise and monitors and headsets, and an energy level that must have been Mach 10. I felt it. The passion of the people in the room. Even Jessica, the lowly intern. And Tyler. Especially Tyler.

"Don't try to be funny," Jessica warned us while we were checking out the soundstage where we'd be interviewed. "AGOAJ hates that. Just talk to him."

"No problem," Tyler said, as if he'd been interviewed a dozen times before.

"I think I'll just skip the talking part and nod and smile," I said.

She laughed. "Not if AGOAJ has his way."

The host went by a string of initials. AGOAJ. It was supposed to be very newsy. He wore a loose-fitting suit over a wifebeater.

He was kind of cute, too. With a smile that made guests forgive him when he twisted the news in an attempt to make it terminally hip.

Tyler picked Jessica's brains about how to get an internship before she left us in the greenroom, which had been supplied with the root beer Tyler liked and the lemonade I drank. Not to mention a bowl full of assorted candy bars and one of popcorn. Hot popcorn.

"This is cool. I could live like this." Tyler didn't mean the greenroom, even though he was unwrapping a Milky Way as he spoke. He meant the news atmosphere. The rush of adrenaline that you could feel in the air here. I suddenly saw him here in a year. It was a weird feeling, seeing him as Tyler the school newspaper editor and then seeing Tyler the college graduate and MTV intern superimposed over the top.

Which, I guess, is the real difference between high school and college. It may be subtle, and it may take a few months to really feel it. But there's only a few years of school between me and a career.

And guess what? I can see Tyler as an

MTV intern, and a news guy. Maybe not as goofy as AGOAJ. But I can't see me as an engineer.

I should have guessed when I didn't get into the whole robot thing with Stephen and Sophia. But I had liked the way "engineer" sounded. And how happy my dad was that I'd have a solid career ahead of me when I graduated.

Which doesn't change the fact that it's just not my passion. And now that I've seen people who pursue their passion— Stephen, Sophia, and even Tyler—I want the same. No matter how safe my parents think a career as an engineer is.

"I'm going to change my major," I said to Tyler.

He just laughed. "I thought you might succumb to the Freshman Switchoff. So what's it going to be?"

"Journalism. I like writing for the paper."

"Hah!" He gave a victory salute. "I knew Mother Hubbard wasn't a quitter!"

"I want to do other things too, besides the column." And this time, I wasn't just saying it because I had a crush on Tyler. I was saying it because I had a crush on journalism.

He didn't seem terribly surprised. "Cool. Maybe you'll be editor in two years."

"Maybe." I wasn't willing to set that goal in stone. I was still way too new at this whole journalism thing. But I liked thinking about it as a possibility.

I don't remember the interview very well. Jessica came and got us from the greenroom and led us on set. Someone else dusted us with powder and fluffed our hair while a third person fit our mics in an efficient and intimate manner. I suppose you get used to it, if you do this for a living. Tyler didn't even seem to mind.

It was the two of us for a minute, just sitting on a soundstage like at an oasis in the desert while cameras and crew swirled around us as the dust settled.

After a minute AGOAJ came onto the set with a brisk move that crackled with every bit of energy I'd felt in this place all day long. He was young. And hotter in person than he was on the TV screen. Definitely buzz factor ten.

The lights came on, someone counted down from three, and suddenly AGOAJ turned to the camera and smiled. "Hello. It isn't just the over-twenty-five crowd who has trouble with dating, love, and relationships. College isn't the greatest place to find 'the one' . . ." He swiveled to face us. "Or is it? Let's ask Mother Goose, shall we?"

"Mother Hubbard," Tyler corrected, blinking in the bright light, and looking from one camera to the other to find the one with the red dot, which was what Jessica had told us to look toward.

AGOAJ smiled, ignoring the correction. "So your Mother Hubbard has the answer for us? Tell me what it is. I could use a little help trying to figure out if my current girlfriend is worth my time?" The audience laughed and he smiled out at them sheepishly. "I'm a busy guy, you know." And then, as if he realized his Neanderthal commentary might not be taken well, he added, "And she's as busy as I am. So I'm wondering for her sake too."

Right. That was his shtick. Terminally hip news meant a little bit of sick humor.

"Mother Hubbard says to go with your instincts," Tyler said. I knew this was the line he'd rehearsed and I was suddenly proud of him for delivering it.

"Well, if that were the case, then I'd be outta there. There's this cute new intern—" He cut himself off with a sideways glance at the camera. "Never mind. Honey, if you're watching this . . . just, never mind."

I wondered if he meant Jessica, who was watching from the sidelines and blushing. But I had no time for that, because all of a sudden ΛGOΛJ was firing a question at me. "As a typical female student at the university, what do you think about the Mother Goose column, Katelyn?"

I had also rehearsed—at Tyler's insistence. "It's made us think about relationships and what works and what hurts." That seemed loud enough and clear enough, I hoped. I wouldn't want to be asked to repeat myself on MTV.

Another few softballs and I was starting to feel really good about the interview. Then he deviated from the list of questions Jessica told us he'd ask. Duh, you'd think I'd be prepared. I had seen the show before.

He looked at me and leaned in sympathetically. "What have you learned from all this? If I'm not getting too personal."

Ooookay. What had I learned? I shrugged. "I've learned that guys have it as rough as we do."

Boring. I could read it on his face. As could the audience. AGOAJ spun away from me toward Tyler.

Tyler shrugged an annoying, *what can you do?* shrug between guys. "Yeah." He nodded like a bobblehead doll; his nerves were apparently getting to him. "You think the girls have all the power—come to find out, they think you have it." The audience laughed.

AGOAJ grinned and seemed pleased that Tyler had managed to inject humor without resorting to the verboten canned jokes. Which, naturally, meant that he wanted to continue along that line of thought. "So, who really has the power?"

Tyler fumbled for a moment, blinking into the lights, and then smiled. I could see him relax. He thought he had this answer nailed. "You'll have to ask Mother Hubbard."

Lame. And AGOAJ wasn't going to let him get away with it either. "Oh come on, she's not here. I'm asking you."

We were both deer in the headlights—or spotlights, more accurately.

For some reason AGOAJ had decided to let us swing. He smiled as he waited for an answer, his eyes widening in delight at every second of dead air, and I felt pressure to answer. But what to say? I guess the first thing that came to mind. "Whoever blinks first has the power."

I meant it in more ways than one. And I'm not even sure what I meant, really.

But the audience roared with agreement. And AGOAJ nodded.

One of the people off screen waved to indicate our segment was out of time, and AGOAJ turned to the audience. "We'll be right back with our youth analyst, Joseph Butler, with a segment on AARP: Friend or Foe."

The friendly faces turned harried and the energy became a wind at our back. We were hustled off the soundstage and out into a narrow hallway.

After a push toward the door at the end

of the hallway, we got the message. We started walking slowly, as if maybe we weren't really even here. As if we hadn't just been on TV. "Looks like we're done."

"Yeah. Except we still have to figure out who's going to blink first."

We were done. Our fifteen minutes had been exactly fifteen minutes. And I was glad.

I took his arm and put it around me. "Let's try to get bounced from one of the hot clubs again."

He pulled away a little and then with a sigh, stopped resisting. "I guess you want me to blink first."

Guys. Do they have to have everything explained to them? "I blinked first."

He tightened his arm around my shoulder. "You did? When?"

"Last night. When I called you. Remember?"

"Oh?" He grinned sheepishly. "I guess I'm a little dense." He looked back down the long hallway. "Or maybe just a little overwhelmed. Did that seem real to you? Or did we just dream it?"

I laughed. "All I remember is bright

lights and babbling. But somehow, I don't think we revealed any secrets—personal, paper, or of the universe, either."

He stopped me. "To them. But if you blinked first, then—"

"Then you know my secret. I leaned up against him and kissed him. "I blinked first. I've had a crush on you since the very first day I met you—when you were following Sophia around like a largemouth bass."

I kissed him again. "I'm willing to see where this goes. But if you decide to run away with some smart Italian girl, do me a favor and tell me so. Don't just fade into the night without ending things."

"Never happen." Tyler leaned forward. "Don't forget, you may have blinked first, but I blinked back." He kissed me and I had no doubt that he had blinked me right out of sidekick mode and into girlfriend status. No ifs, ands, or buts about it.

So why did that feel scary and cool and a bit like being on the top of a cliff about to jump off? Well, it meant some of those Mother Hubbard haters had been right. Maybe my third-date rule *had* been a way to avoid that sense of falling too fast and too hard. And to avoid the potentially nasty *splat* if there was no big marshmallow of true love to catch me.

Oh well, marshmallow or not, I was jumping. Mother Hubbard might have disapproved, but I liked it. What's life if we never gamble a little, anyway?

I guess Tyler could tell I had lost focus on the kiss because he pulled away. "Don't tell me you're thinking about how you'll rate me in your little pink book?" He looked around at the bland white hallway leading away from the fantasy world of MTV (that might one day turn to reality for him). "How could any rating book capture all this?"

He had a point. Tyler definitely registered off the excitement meter. Think about it—we'd been on TV. We'd seen what a greenroom looked like. Okay. It was nothing remarkable. Although it did have good food.

But should I let him know I hadn't been thinking about little pink books or rating systems? I had just decided to jump headfirst off the cliff of love, after all. My mind was far from a book full of bad dates. So I said flippantly, "What little pink book?"

He grinned as he swept open the big metal doors that led out of the studio and into the noise and bustle of New York City. "I guess that means I hit the ten spots in every category."

"Oh, I don't know about that," I said coyly. Then I took a deep breath. "Okay. I'm throwing out the stupid third-date rule from now on. I mean, who needs a little pink book when I have you?"

I think I shocked him. He stood there in the open doorway, blinking in surprise. "Really? You'd throw it away? For me?"

Interesting. I wasn't the only scared one. "Of course."

"Then give it here." He pointed to my backpack. "I want to see what you rated me." He grinned. "And what you called me. I'm guessing Man of My Dreams."

"In your dreams." I didn't make a move to open my backpack. "Besides, I never put you in there."

I didn't give him a chance to argue, I just kissed him out the door and into the street, where we were nearly run down by a pack of briefcase-toting commuters heading for the subway.

Some guy snarled, "Hey, get a room!"

We were feeling so good we just laughed. Besides, the guy was already lost in the fast-moving crowd.

We walked into Times Square and stood looking up at the big display screen where we'd been featured just yesterday. Tyler squeezed my hand. "Can you believe we were up there yesterday? It doesn't seem real, does it?"

"No." I leaned my head on his shoulder. "But it was." Sure, no one but us would probably ever know or care that our giant pictures had once graced Times Square for a day. But we would never forget.

"Are you sure I'm not in that book?"

"Yup." I lied. I squeezed his hand gently, though, so he wouldn't know. After all, it was better for both of us if he never knew he'd been in my book all along under the nickname The Drooling Fool. "And I'm going to burn it. Haven't you heard? Little black books are so passé. Even when they come in hot pink."

He kissed me. "Burning's good. After all, how many guys like me are there in the world?"

Right. I'd reserve judgment on that for at least the next three and a half years.

I guess some people are like Sophia and Stephen. They see what they like and they go for it. They don't let anything get in their way.

People like Tyler and me, we are a little more cautious, more careful with our feelings. We need time to adjust. But we get there—eventually. And when we do . . . well, suffice it to say, it was like New Year's Eve right there in Times Square. If I *were* to keep my little pink book, it would say buzz factor ten for Tyler, no doubt.

Eventually, though, I'd learn that shortly after your crush turns into a relationship, the buzz goes away. But don't worry. A nice warm glow takes its place. And that lasts for a long, long time.

About the Author

Kelly McClymer was born in South Carolina, but crossed the Mason-Dixon line to live in Delaware at age six. After one short stint living in South Carolina during junior high, she has remained above the line, and now lives in Maine with her husband and three children.

Writing has been Kelly's passion since her sixth grade essay on how not to bake bread earned her an A plus. After cleaning up the bread dough that oozed onto the floor, she gave up bread making for good and turned to writing as a creative outlet. A graduate of the University of Delaware (English major, of course), she spends her days writing and teaching writing. Look for her next book, *The Salem Witch Tryouts*, from Simon Pulse in Fall 2006.

WANTED

Single Teen Reader in search of a FUN romantic comedy read!

Available from Simon Pulse Published by Simon & Schuster